Jessica pushed   and immediately felt t   inds were drawn, and   ose shade had been c   terial. Ryan was lying across his bed, his tanned, muscular body bare except for a skimpy square-cut bathing suit. In the dim light his body glowed like a Greek god's.

"Jessica," he exclaimed, sitting up. "What a surprise. Come on in. I'm glad to see you."

Jessica stumbled into the small room, her eyes glued to Ryan's powerful swimmer's physique. "I'm glad to see you too," she managed, falling squarely onto a rickety wooden stool a few feet from his bed. She widened her eyes in mock astonishment. "And so much of you."

Ryan threw back his head and laughed. "That's what I love about you, Jessica—you're always quick." He lay back on his bed, stretching his hands behind his head, his biceps flexing. "You obviously know how to have a good time."

Jessica ran a slender hand through her long blond hair and gave him a sly look. "Fun's my middle name."

Ryan patted the checkered bedspread beside him. "Wouldn't you be more comfortable sitting here?"

Jessica gulped. *I'll say,* she thought, slipping her hands, palms down, beneath her thighs and sitting on them. *But I have a feeling I'll get in a lot less trouble if I stay over here.*

Bantam Books in the Sweet Valley University series.
Ask your bookseller for the books you have missed.

And don't miss these Sweet Valley
University Thriller Editions:

Visit the Official Sweet Valley Web Site on the Internet at:

http://www.sweetvalley.com

SWEET VALLEY UNIVERSITY®

The Truth About Ryan

Written by
Laurie John

Created by
FRANCINE PASCAL

BANTAM BOOKS
NEW YORK · TORONTO · LONDON · SYDNEY · AUCKLAND

RL 6, age 12 and up

THE TRUTH ABOUT RYAN

A Bantam Book / August 1997

Sweet Valley High® *and Sweet Valley University*®
are registered trademarks of Francine Pascal.
Conceived by Francine Pascal.
Produced by Daniel Weiss Associates, Inc.
33 West 17th Street
New York, NY 10011.

ISBN: 0-553-57055-2

Published simultaneously in the United States and Canada

*Bantam Books are published by Bantam Books, a division of Bantam
Doubleday Dell Publishing Group, Inc. Its trademark, consisting of the
words "Bantam Books" and the portrayal of a rooster, is Registered in
U.S. Patent and Trademark Office and in other countries. Marca
Registrada. Bantam Books, 1540 Broadway, New York, New York 10036.*

PRINTED IN THE UNITED STATES OF AMERICA

OPM   0 9 8 7 6 5 4 3 2 1

To Jane Elizabeth Chardiet

Chapter One

"Where *are* you, Ryan Taylor?" Elizabeth Wakefield whispered, squeezing the receiver of the service station's pay phone in her slender hand. The answering machine on the other end of the line was suggesting she leave a message.

"But I've left a message," she insisted. "I've left at least ten of them since I finally found a working phone last night!"

Elizabeth shuddered, remembering her lonely wait in the deserted rest stop where her Jeep had broken down—and the silence that had greeted her when she'd picked up the broken receiver of the only phone within walking distance. She had flagged down a passerby on the highway, who thankfully had driven her into town and called a service station for her. The Jeep that Elizabeth shared with her twin sister had finally been towed in the dark of night, and Elizabeth along with it. She had been at the garage ever since. But where in the world was her AWOL boyfriend?

"Ryan, this is Elizabeth," she said urgently after she heard the beep. "If you're there, please pick up. I'm sorry—" *Click.* The machine cut her off.

"Aargh!" she cried, slamming down the receiver in disgust. She found another quarter and quickly redialed the number. The phone on the other end rang and rang; it rang way past the four rings that should have activated Ryan's answering machine. *I must have used up his tape,* she realized, frustrated.

Elizabeth gently, resignedly put the receiver back in its hook and turned to face the garage's service area. She took a deep breath to steady her nerves. "I'm sure it won't take them much longer to fix the Jeep," she assured herself. Then she could find Ryan and talk to him face-to-face.

I've got to let him know it wasn't my fault that I stood him up last night, she thought. If the Jeep hadn't broken down, she would have made it to the restaurant in time to meet Ryan and to celebrate another year of his sobriety.

"Let me tell you something, lady," the head mechanic declared, striding over to meet Elizabeth at the pay phone. "You can't push a

2

motor vehicle like you did and not expect trouble. Not with the temperatures we've been having."

Elizabeth sighed, brushing a loose strand of golden blond hair from her face. It was only eight o'clock in the morning. She'd hardly been able to get a few minutes' sleep all night—she didn't feel comfortable taking a nap around those guys in her now-smudged white tank dress and heels. A young mechanic offered her a blanket at one point, but she had been too nervous to stretch out on the hard wooden bench and relax. And now, she realized with dread, she still had a full day of lifeguard duty ahead of her. What she needed was an instant good-night's rest and a fixed Jeep—not a lecture on driving etiquette.

Elizabeth followed the head mechanic into the service area, stepping carefully over a large puddle of oil on the cement floor. The red Jeep stood forlorn in a large, dingy garage. Chrome tools and advertisements for tires, mufflers, and brake pads covered the walls.

"With all the damage you did, it's a good thing you came to *my* service station." He pointed a pudgy, oil-covered finger at his chest. *Ralph* was stenciled in red thread across the left pocket of his grease-stained coveralls. He peered back into the hood of Elizabeth's cherry red Jeep and let out a low whistle.

Elizabeth rolled her aquamarine eyes. "Well,

it's not like I had much of a choice," she muttered. The good Samaritan she had flagged down last night had turned out to be Ralph's brother-in-law.

"If you'd had this baby towed to the place near the highway, you'd be looking at a huge bill. But me, even with all the terrible damage you did—"

"I know. I know," Elizabeth cut in. She couldn't stand to hear any more about how badly she'd punished the Jeep. All she wanted was to get in touch with Ryan and make sure he was all right. *Could Ryan have run off again, like he did last summer?* a voice in her head asked.

Despite the eighty-degree heat the chilling thought of Ryan disappearing from her life raised goose bumps on Elizabeth's tawny limbs. She wrapped her arms around herself and shivered despite the oncoming heat. *What a ridiculous thought,* she chided herself. *Ryan has no reason to run away. Last summer he didn't want me to know he was a recovering alcoholic. But now that I know, I support his sobriety a hundred percent.* She turned back to the mechanic. "How quickly can you fix my Jeep?"

The mechanic shrugged and pulled a wrench from his tool belt. "Couple of days. A week, tops."

"What?" Elizabeth gasped. "Oh no! That's impossible!"

The mechanic leaned over the hood of the Jeep. "There's a lot to fix. What were you doing anyway? Racing to a fire?"

Elizabeth narrowed her eyes. "I was in a hurry," she snapped. "And I still am. Can't you speed it up? I'm a lifeguard at Sweet Valley Shore, and I have to be at my post *now!* Plus I . . . I need to check in on a friend too. It's an emergency."

The mechanic straightened up, shaking his head. "We got a broken fan belt and a leaky radiator, not to mention a couple of blown hoses. I hope it was a matter of life and death and not a case of being late for a date because you spent too much time at the beauty parlor."

Elizabeth's blue-green eyes flashed angrily. *What a typical sexist remark,* she thought. Then she felt her cheeks flush a hot red when she realized that was *exactly* what had happened last night. "How did you know that?" she demanded.

The mechanic gave her a kindly chuckle and shrugged. "Happens all the time. Half my business comes from ladies spending too much time at the beauty parlor. You'd think I was in cahoots with the salons, if you knew the amount of money I make." He ran his hands across the front of his coveralls and left two greasy smears. "But it's a shame to see what happens to the cars."

"I'll have you know it was *extremely* important.

My boyfriend had an anniversary to celebrate last night, and he was counting on me."

"Lady." The mechanic laughed, wiping his face with a soiled rag. "Spare me your love life. I just fix cars."

Elizabeth turned away, fuming. "Staying sober for any amount of time is an amazing feat," she murmured. "More than that man will ever know. I would have driven my Jeep into the ground to be there for Ryan."

But maybe Ryan doesn't realize that, Elizabeth thought with a start. *All he knows for sure is that I didn't show up.*

A sinking sensation gripped Elizabeth's belly. "I let him down," she whispered. "Just when he needed me most." A sob caught in her throat. Being stood up might not have been so bad if Patti, Ryan's Alcoholics Anonymous sponsor, would have been there for him. But Patti had recently gone back to the bottle, and she was practically encouraging Ryan to do the same.

That must seem like the ultimate betrayal, Elizabeth thought. And now, for all Ryan knew, Elizabeth had betrayed him too.

"But I didn't, Ryan," she whispered. "I tried to make it for our date last night. I tried so hard that I—"

"Overheated the engine and broke the fan belt," the mechanic cut in, holding up a long piece of rubber that looked slightly scorched at one end.

Elizabeth sniffed, feeling a little indignant at having been overheard by the mechanic. "It wasn't my fault. If Nina hadn't made me work her shift at the beach, I could have had my hair done in time and I wouldn't have had to rush."

"See what I mean?" The mechanic chortled. "It's always the beauty parlor. It ruins more cars and busts up more relationships. So let me give you a word of advice—"

"Thanks, but no thanks." Elizabeth tossed her long blond ponytail over her shoulder. "You fix the Jeep. I'll take care of my own relationships. Now, if you'll excuse me, I need to use your phone again. Apparently I'm going to need a taxi!"

"Leave me alone!" Ryan Taylor roared from the tangled sheets of his bed. The phone seemed unbelievably loud in the small living quarters he kept at the back of the main lifeguard tower. He grabbed his pillow and covered his head, desperately trying to muffle the noise. *Brrring, brrring,* the phone howled.

Stop ringing, he commanded mentally, but without success. The tape on the answering machine was obviously full. And the timing couldn't have been worse. The sound was setting his teeth on edge.

Ryan knew of only one person in the world who

could be so persistent: Elizabeth Wakefield, his so-called girlfriend. First she couldn't be bothered to show up to celebrate his anniversary of sobriety last night. Now she was bombarding the answering machine with her lame excuses. *What a fool I was to think that she cared about me,* he thought.

He opened one swollen eyelid and immediately regretted it. The bright California sun was streaming through the cracks in the shutters, nearly blinding him. His brain was pounding like a twenty-one-gun salute. He gingerly turned his head to face the screaming phone. The image of two phones, superimposed on each other, swam toward him in a sickening dance. He was about to start the slow crawl across the floor to yank the cord from the wall when the ringing mercifully stopped. He breathed a sigh of relief.

A nagging thought flitted across his tired brain. *You drank last night, Ryan. You drank too much.*

"Bull," he spat back, propping himself up on his powerful arms, ignoring the shock waves that hammered through his muscular body down to his toes. "I didn't drink enough. I had a lot of wasted time to celebrate. A lot of lies. When the people who were supposed to care about me showed their true colors, I had a lot of dryness to make up for!"

He fell back onto his bed, causing the perfectly

chiseled features of his face to scrunch up in pain. Just then the phone began its shrill, piercing ring again. His temples became a vise, squeezing his head and turning the dull ache behind his eyes into an unbearable torture. He lunged out, sweeping the phone off the small rattan table by his bedside. "Enough with your noise, Elizabeth," he shouted. "You drove me to drink. Now leave me in peace!"

Suddenly in his mind's eye the face of a pretty, red-haired woman loomed before him. "You know that's not true, Ryan," she told him softly. "No one is responsible for your drinking but yourself. You can't blame Elizabeth."

A lone tear squeezed from Ryan's bloodshot eye. "Patti." He whispered the woman's name. His A.A. sponsor had said a lot of things in the past that had helped him stay sober. But then the image was replaced by another, more recent one. Patti popping open a can of beer at dinner the other night. *"Lighten up,"* her voice echoed. *"Why shouldn't you have a drink once in a while? You and I can both handle it."*

Ryan flung his pillow across the room. "You see?" he screamed at the surfing posters covering the thin walls. "It's all worthless now. If Patti can drink, then so can I."

He struggled to his feet, the motion causing his stomach to lurch wildly. He looked down to steady himself. "Oh," he groaned. He was still wearing the oxford dress shirt, tie, and dark suit he'd worn the night before. Now they were a rumpled, sweaty mess.

Sleeping in your clothes, Ryan? a sneering voice in his head asked.

"What if I did?" he bellowed. "Right now all I want is a drink!" He stumbled toward the bureau, an insatiable urge for alcohol overwhelming every one of his senses. "This one's on you, Elizabeth. If you hadn't been hounding me with phone calls, I could have been sleeping off this hangover. Now what I need is a little hair of the dog."

He wrenched open the top drawer, throwing his socks and underwear onto the floor as he rummaged to the back. "Where is it?" he muttered. He pulled open the middle drawer, dumping its contents and kicking his T-shirts and swim trunks aside with his foot. "Where?" he cried.

Suddenly he turned as if possessed and ran out of his bedroom into the small alcove of the kitchen. He yanked open the utility cupboard above the stove where he kept his tools. "Ahh." He smiled, pushing aside a wrench. "There you are."

Ryan chuckled to himself. Even though he lived alone, old habits died hard. He'd hidden the bottle of whiskey last night—like any active alcoholic who didn't want to get caught. He smiled as he held it up to the light. Still half full. "I'm a lightweight," he said with a laugh. "Two years ago I would have polished this bottle off in one sitting and started on a new one."

And failed to show up for work as a result, a small voice—Patti's voice, the old Patti—reminded him. An anguished vein began to pound in his temple. And then the blue-tinged face of Kelly Anne O'Dwyer flashed across his memory. Just a couple of summers before, Ryan had passed out during an all-night bender. A rookie lifeguard had taken his shift. Kelly Anne was a five-year-old girl who'd been playing in the surf when a riptide cut through a section of the beach—a full swingback tidal shift that only an experienced pro would have been able to read and handle. The rookie had been unable to save the child, but Ryan could have. If only he'd been there . . . if only he'd been sober.

Ryan hung his head. "It's not my fault," he cried, gripping the whiskey bottle. "Everybody expects me to be there for them. But who's there for me? Nobody! Except you." He swung the bottle to his lips and took a long, healthy slug. The liquid burned a hot trail down his throat, and he had to swallow hard to keep his stomach from rebelling. Almost immediately, though, his mind began to relax. Patti, Elizabeth, even the image of little Kelly Anne began to fade.

11

"To me," he slurred, raising the bottle to his bleary-eyed reflection in the cabinet's polished surface. "To me and my pal, whiskey. You're all I'll ever need."

"What a fabulous morning!" Jessica Wakefield exclaimed. She flung open her large bedroom window and took a deep, satisfying gulp of the fragrant salt air that was being carried in on the ocean breeze. "Home, sweet summer home."

She was thrilled to have the same large attic room in the three-story Victorian beach house that she'd lived in last summer. This year she was only sharing the house with her twin sister, Elizabeth, their friend Nina Harper, and Ben Mercer—Jessica's sexy, hard-bodied boyfriend from the previous summer. Their other two housemates from last summer, Winston Egbert and Wendy Wolman Paloma, were staying in the spacious Paloma beach house across town.

Jessica twirled around and caught her reflection in the full-length mahogany mirror. "Hi, gorgeous," she murmured approvingly. Her tight red miniskirt and white halter top showed off her slender curves to perfection. "I guess I could have saved myself a lot of trouble and just worn my lifeguard suit," she mused, studying herself up and down. "I *do* have to work today. But. . ."

she shrugged. "Ben's never seen this outfit."

She grabbed her backpack and quickly shoved in her red lifeguard swimsuit, her regulation white nylon jacket, her whistle, a bottle of sunscreen, and her Sweet Valley Shore cap. She would change in the main lifeguard tower for her shift at the beach. She skipped toward the door, ignoring the clothes she had scattered across the massive wooden captain's bed that dominated the room.

"I'll deal with that mess later," she reasoned, tossing one last look at her trashed room. She had more important things to take care of—like checking in on Ben Mercer, who was always up first thing in the morning.

Jessica slung the backpack over her shoulder and bounced happily out of her bedroom toward the polished wooden staircase that led downstairs. This was the first really good mood she'd been in since arriving at Sweet Valley Shore and finding, to her extreme humiliation, that Ben had brought along his new girlfriend. She'd thought winning Ben back would be as easy as snapping her fingers. But prying him away from Priya Rahman was proving a lot more difficult than she'd expected.

Last summer Jessica couldn't get away from Ben no matter how hard she tried. Even when she'd pretended that her crush on head lifeguard Ryan Taylor was mutual, Ben had refused to take no for an answer.

13

Jessica cringed, remembering how *that* had blown up in her face. Ryan had only been interested in her lifeguarding abilities. It was her twin sister, Elizabeth, who he'd had his romantic eye on.

And now Ben's distracted too, Jessica thought with a derisive snort. She wrinkled her pretty nose as she remembered the first time she'd seen Priya running across the beach, her long, dark hair streaming behind her. Jessica gripped the banister in a spasm of anger as she recalled how Ben's bright blue eyes had lit up at the sight. There were few girls who could hold a candle to Jessica's tanned, golden beauty and slim, athletic body. Unfortunately Priya was one of them— but not for long.

Even Jessica's identical twin, Elizabeth, lacked the special spark that twinkled in Jessica's eyes and drew guys to her like moths to a flame. She had superior fashion know-how and personal flair—and also a deep commitment to fun. Elizabeth's pursuits tended toward the more serious aspects of life—work, study, and more work. Whether it was her job as ace reporter at Sweet Valley University or her hectic course load, Elizabeth was always busy. Jessica's main interests on the same campus were good-looking guys and having great times. She was used to being the most sought-after woman in a crowd. And getting any man she wanted.

Until Priya came along, Jessica thought despondently, stepping into the living room. She sank down onto the soft cushions of the magenta-and-white-striped canvas sofa, letting her backpack slip off her shoulder. She wasn't quite ready to face Ben yet. She brushed a strand of golden blond hair from her face. "Priya isn't just beautiful," she growled to herself. "She's smart too."

Jessica grabbed a matching magenta pillow and held it to her chest, cringing as she remembered Ben's remarks about how *intellectual* and *bright* and *intelligent* Priya was.

He as much as said that our affair last summer was nothing more than a dull distraction, she thought angrily. She punched the pillow. "Priya loved that," she spat, remembering Priya's triumphant smile. "There's nothing that girl likes better than showing off her brains at my expense!"

Until yesterday, Jessica thought, a sly smile spreading across her face. *I threw Priya a zinger so hot that even Ben was impressed!*

"Miss Know-it-all thought she was so clever." Jessica smirked. "But you don't need to be a bookworm if you go to a few movies." And being one of Keanu Reeves's many number-one fans, she knew his performance as Danceny in *Dangerous Liaisons* inside and out. Priya's dark

15

brown eyes had turned a furious black when Jessica pointed out that Priya had gotten Danceny mixed up with another character from the classic French story. "Maybe I'll take all of next semester off and spend it at the multiplex," Jessica quipped gleefully.

She stood up and smoothed down the front of her miniskirt, leaving her backpack by the sofa. *I'm ready now,* she thought, starting for the kitchen. She grinned widely as she pushed through the swinging doors.

Ben was sitting at the large wooden table in the middle of the kitchen, his left hand wrapped around a mug of steaming coffee. The Monday morning newspaper was spread out before him.

"Ben!" Jessica chirped. "Fancy finding you here."

Ben tipped back his maroon University of Chicago baseball cap and fixed her with one bright blue eye before ducking back to his paper. "I *do* live here," he replied with dry sarcasm.

Jessica ignored his tone and continued to smile as she poured herself a mug of coffee. "I guess I just *assumed,*" she said sweetly, her own sarcasm dripping with sugar, "that you'd be having breakfast with Priya. Or perhaps her dreary summaries of books by dead Russians have finally started to bore you." She slipped into the seat across from him.

Ben shook his head as he looked up from the table, a lock of dark hair spilling into his face. "Hardly, Jessica. Priya's understanding of Dostoyevsky's *Crime and Punishment* could keep me in rapture for years."

Oh, puh-leeze, Jessica thought, glowering as she roughly stirred some milk into her mug. She'd tried to read that book. All Dostoyevsky had done for her was give her a headache. The last thing Jessica wanted to do right now was have a quaint little literary chat. What was Ben's problem anyway? After the admiring way he'd looked at her, she thought she'd have him under her well-manicured thumb.

An idea came to her in a flash. She put down her mug and got up from her chair, walking around to stand behind him. "You look tense, Ben," she murmured sexily.

His paper rustled as he rigidly turned the pages. "I'm fine," he mumbled.

"No, really," Jessica purred. She slid her slender fingers around his broad, muscular shoulders. "I know just the thing to help you relax." She began to massage his powerful back through the soft cotton of his T-shirt. But instead of feeling his muscles relax, she could feel the knots in his back tightening with every passing squeeze.

Ben twisted away from her. "What do you

think you're doing?" His handsome face was locked in a scowl.

Jessica took a step back, shocked. "I was just . . . I thought that you . . ."

Ben shook his head, his lip curled in disbelief. "Forget it, Jessica. I'm in love with Priya. Sure, you got in one good crack last night, but that doesn't win the war."

Jessica's mouth dropped open. *How dare you!* her mind raged. She felt her face flush a hot crimson. "Ben Mercer, you're the most conceited, arrogant, stuck-up loser I've ever met!"

Ben broke out into peals of laughter. "Takes one to know one, Jessica. And by the way, Priya has that same miniskirt . . . except on her, it doesn't pucker around the thighs."

Jessica stared down at her skirt. It *was* a fraction of an inch too tight. So what?

"I hate you, Ben Mercer," she screeched, running from the room. "I'll get you back if it's the last thing I do!"

"Can you feel it, Nina?" Stu Kirkwood asked in his deep, mellow drawl.

"Hmmm?" Nina Harper stood facing Stu in the soft, sandy dunes of the beach. Just a few yards beyond the dunes was the Victorian beach house she called her summer home. If Nina was slightly distracted, it was only because Stu

18

looked so incredibly sexy in the light of the early morning. The gentle sea breeze ruffled his long, sun-streaked blond hair; the locks glinted like gold in the rising sun.

"Can you feel how the energy is traveling between us, like a warm glow?" Stu asked.

Nina nodded, feeling her straightened black hair brushing her shoulders. She was amazed at the powerful energy being generated between her and Stu's open palms. *And we aren't even touching,* she thought. She gazed tenderly into his eyes, lost in their tranquil, blue confidence.

"It's beautiful," she gushed, hardly believing those words had come from her usually matter-of-fact lips. *Who is this girl anyway?* she wondered, smiling contentedly. She'd changed since the day she'd washed ashore at Stu's cool adobe beach house on SeaMist Island at the beginning of the summer. She was no longer the serious, overanalytical Nina who was scornful of anything that even hinted at "alternative" and "New Age." Now she was a new, open, and receptive Nina who had a deepening sense of the world's spirituality and a new, sensitive awareness.

As she stood a few feet from Stu, her arms outspread, wordlessly transferring energy, she felt calm and whole and in total sync with nature. She was aware of her bare feet in the soft white sand, the warm ocean breeze fluttering her short peach-colored sundress, the sweet smell of lilac bushes that lined the side of the beach house, and the muffled cry of gulls far out over the pier. She was at peace.

Stu dropped his palms first. "That was awesome," he whispered. "I've never felt such a powerful connection with anyone. I really think we were meant to be together. Don't you?"

Nina felt herself blush and pulled back slightly. The idea scared her. She'd only been at Sweet Valley Shore for a little while. How could she already be going back on her promise that this summer was strictly no-guys? To let herself fall for Stu was strictly forbidden.

She dropped her eyes to her bare toes and watched as they curled in the warm sand. She was still smarting over what Bryan Nelson, her boyfriend from Sweet Valley University, had done to her.

Ex-boyfriend, Nina thought, remembering how she had called Bryan in Washington, D.C., late at night before she left for Sweet Valley Shore. It hadn't been Bryan's deep voice that answered his phone—but a woman's!

Nina swallowed hard and let her dark, chocolate brown eyes travel back to where Stu was standing patiently, wearing his heart practically on his sleeve. If ever there was the perfect man for her, it was him.

Smiling, Nina remembered the conversation

she'd had with Jessica the night they'd arrived at Sweet Valley Shore. Nina had, without really thinking about it, told Jessica that her "perfect man" would stand six-foot three and have gorgeous calves, a small tattoo, a sweet and easygoing personality, and unflagging faithfulness to the degree of his having to live on a deserted island so he'd be distracted by no other women. Stu had turned out to be all those things and more—right down to the inconspicuous yin and yang tattoo that decorated his bicep and the remote island on which he'd built his own home.

"Oh, Stu," Nina purred softly, avoiding his question. "It was fantastic. Thanks for waking me up for the sunrise."

Stu smiled and tucked his long blond hair behind his ears. "And you said you thought mornings were a total bummer."

Nina giggled. "They are, usually. But I wouldn't have missed this for the world."

Stu reached out and pulled her toward him, kissing her softly on the tip of the nose. "I was hoping you'd feel that way," he murmured, gazing deeply into her eyes.

Nina felt her insides begin to melt. She took a deep breath.

"Hey, are you OK?" Stu asked, his forehead wrinkling in concern.

Nina laughed and fanned herself. "A little hot."

Stu hugged her. "I know what will cool you down. We'll go for a swim. Look at that water—hardly a ripple. I love the ocean in the early morning. That's when the sea is at its most gentle."

"And you call yourself a surfer?" Nina teased.

Stu grinned. "That's different. When I have my board and my wet suit, I want radical curls. But with my ultimate babe"—he hugged Nina again—"I want it calm and peaceful. Just the two of us floating around in Mother Nature's cradle. See how it's almost calling to us?"

Nina turned her attention to the shore. As a lifeguard she was used to studying the water, but as an adversary, not a friend. Her job was saving lives; that meant constantly fighting the sea, always being wary. But now she felt as if she were seeing the ocean through Stu's eyes.

He's right, she realized, watching the waves lap gently at the shore, leaving their lacy white foam behind. A swim was an excellent idea. *Too bad I didn't come prepared,* she thought, glancing down at Stu's attire. He was always ready for a dip in the ocean, practically living in his old cutoffs and faded T-shirts.

"That sounds perfect, Stu. I'll just run in and change."

"Why bother?" he asked, looking up and down the deserted beach. "No one's around."

Nina giggled nervously and shook her head. She might be developing a newfound spiritual awareness, but she hadn't changed *that* much. Skinny-dipping in broad daylight was not about to become part of the Nina Harper repertoire. "Like I said, I'll go change."

"Cool. Whatever you're comfortable with," Stu said with a smile, dropping down cross-legged on the sand to wait for her.

What a sweet guy, Nina thought happily as she bounded up the stairs to her bedroom on the second floor of the beach house. *For an incredibly successful business tycoon, he's completely laid-back. Who would believe he's a millionaire?*

Some time ago Stu had created TubeRiders, a surfboard customized for his own needs, and unwittingly parlayed it into a business empire that had earned him more money than he'd ever dreamed of. But he was hardly the businessman type; all he wanted to do was sit by the beach and commune peacefully with nature or go out on the waves and surf. So he'd sold part of the business to a partner who would handle the day-to-day stuff while he lived the life of a king. And for Stu, that was hardly anything more indulgent than the large, secluded adobe beach house he'd built for himself, complete with a private bridge connecting SeaMist Island to the mainland.

My dream man, Nina thought, starting when she

suddenly heard Jessica and Ben's raised voices from downstairs. "Sounds like a real fight to me," Nina muttered, running to the landing just in time to see Jessica storm out through the front door. Ben followed close at her heels, laughing sardonically.

Nina sighed. "There go two people who could use some energy transference," she mused, walking back into her brightly painted bedroom. The sunny yellow walls always made her feel especially happy. She opened her antique cherry-wood dresser and rummaged through the bottom drawer for her favorite bikini.

"I hope Stu isn't too calm, cool, or collected when he sees me in this suit," she murmured, envisioning herself in the gold two-piece. The color beautifully set off her soft ebony skin and the cut showed off her toned, flat tummy.

"Oh, no," she gasped, stepping back and holding the bikini up in front of the bureau's mirror. There was a huge tear in the bikini's bottom, and the top looked as if it had been chewed up by a Jet Ski propeller.

Did I put this in the dryer by accident? she wondered in horror. She knew her mind had been occupied with thoughts of Stu lately, but she couldn't believe she'd become *that* careless.

"Oh, well." Nina sighed, tossing the bathing suit onto her flowered bedspread. "I guess I'll wear the blue one-piece." But as her hand went toward the familiar blue Lycra shoulder strap, she knew something was wrong. Her blue bathing suit had been practically ripped apart too!

"What *is* this?" Nina cried, pulling her other bathing suits from the drawer. All of them, even her red lifeguard suits, were in tatters. "Is this some kind of perverse joke?" Sure, she'd played her own share of practical jokes in her time, but this was sick. She was just about to call a house meeting when she remembered that both Jessica and Ben had just left. And she had gotten a message late last night from Elizabeth, who was going to be stuck at a garage for who knew how long getting the Jeep fixed.

Nina peered more closely at the damaged bathing suits. "They look like they've been slashed with a knife . . . or maybe a razor blade," she whispered, examining them one by one.

Suddenly the tiny hairs on the back of her neck stood up. *If no one is here,* she thought, *then how come I have the distinct impression I'm not alone?*

"Stu?" she called softly, tentatively. But as she whirled around to check behind her, she felt a loud crack reverberate through her head. Then everything went black.

Chapter Two

"Ow!" Winston Egbert cried, biting down on his throbbing knuckle to alleviate the pain. He leaned back dejectedly in the red vinyl booth at the Sea Breeze diner and adjusted his aviator glasses. "Why'd you do that?"

Wendy Paloma rolled her light gray eyes. She still held her knuckle-rapping fork at the ready. "Winston, that's *my* breakfast. You have plenty of food on your plate."

Winston sheepishly shrugged his bony, Hawaiian-shirt-clad shoulders. "I know. But when I'm finished with my eggs and bacon, I'll still be hungry. I just wanted to eat some of your pancakes before they got cold."

Wendy shook her head and giggled. "That doesn't make any sense."

"But I'm a growing boy," Winston whined.

"See how tall and thin I am?" He stood up and sucked in his stomach. Then he wiggled his hips and did the twist so that his khaki pants slipped down a notch. It always worked with his mother.

"Growing *outward*," Wendy teased. "Every morning there's half as much food in the house as the night before, so I know you're making midnight raids on the refrigerator." She reached over the Formica table to pinch his belly.

"Stop it," Winston gasped. "I'm ticklish." As he fended off her attempts to squeeze him he grabbed the last piece of her blueberry muffin and popped it into his mouth.

"Winston!" Wendy cried. "I was going to eat that."

"Well, now you're not." Winston smirked and dropped back down into the booth. "You've got to be fast where Quick-draw Egbert is concerned. Didn't you read my contract? Whenever I accept a gracious offer to stay at a friend's house for the entire summer, full food rights are included. It's in the fine print."

"This is an outrage," Wendy cried in mock indignation. "I'm taking you to small-friends court!"

Winston laughed. "I guess my behavior makes you miss Pedro even more," he said good-naturedly, glad for the opportunity to talk about Wendy's superstar husband. "I bet he lets you eat in peace."

Suddenly a dark cloud seemed to descend over Wendy. It took all the sparkle out of her eyes. Sniffling, she pushed her barely touched plate of food toward him. "You finish it, Winnie. I'm not hungry anyway."

Winston felt his stomach drop to the floor. "I'm sorry, Wendy. I didn't mean to upset you. Maybe we should talk about it." For hours Winston had wanted to bring up the subject of her husband, but Wendy had always seemed too aloof or too guarded.

Wendy cradled her face in her slender hands. Her glossy, shoulder-length, artistically cut brown hair swung forward to hide her expression. "There's nothing to say, really. I never like to eat much in the morning anyway."

Winston sighed as he stared at Wendy's wall of hair. There was plenty to say, and he knew it. The previous evening Wendy had dropped a bombshell on him. She was thinking of divorcing Pedro Paloma, the superstar singer and the man of her dreams. Over the course of the previous summer Wendy had gone from being Pedro's biggest fan to Pedro's fiancée. But now things had turned sour—and Winston couldn't believe it. After all, he was the one who had brought the seemingly perfect couple together. *Something isn't right here*, Winston thought, *and as her friend, it's up to me to get to the bottom of it.*

Wendy shifted in the booth and took a sip of her coffee. "Did I tell you about Miss Storey, my English professor?"

Winston nodded. "Twice." He didn't mean to be rude, but he didn't want the subject to change again. All morning Wendy had been chatting about the weather, her college classes, even Winston's latest disaster in the job front—everything but Pedro. "Look, I think we should talk about—"

Wendy suddenly jumped to her feet and knocked over her water glass, splashing the front of her blue-and-white-striped designer sundress. "Waitress," she cried out. "Could I have more coffee?"

Winston grabbed her lightly tanned arm. "Wendy, you still have half a cup. Sit down and tell me what's going on."

Wendy collapsed back down into the booth and began dabbing at her dress with a napkin. "I'm sorry. This is really hard for me." Her eyes misted over, and for a moment Winston was afraid she was going to cry. But instead she swallowed hard and faced him. "I don't know where to begin," she said in a small voice. "Everything was great in the beginning. Remember how happy I was at the end of last summer?"

Winston nodded and ran a hand through his mop of unruly brown curls. It had been touch and go there at the beginning of the summer.

Wendy had been furious when she'd found out that Pedro had only asked her out for their first date because Winston had threatened to bring hoards of tourists to gape at his house if he didn't. So it had taken a lot for Pedro to convince Wendy that a second date was really his idea—a florist shop full of flowers to be precise! *But in the end,* Winston thought, *Wendy made a radiant bride.*

Wendy toyed with the rim of her coffee cup. "Since Pedro's new album came out, he's been on the road all the time. Before you came to stay with me for the summer, I was talking to the walls, just to hear a human voice."

"Couldn't you go with him?" Winston asked.

Wendy shook her head. "I tried that. But I faded into the background like a stage prop. As far as his tour manager and entourage were concerned, I was just another piece of equipment that had to get moved from city to city."

"But . . . but . . . ," Winston stammered, searching for a way to comfort her. "At least you would have a chance to be together, right?"

Wendy shook her head tiredly. "When Pedro's on tour, he's working. He doesn't always have the time or energy to be with me anymore." Wendy sighed and twisted her napkin. "If I can't really be with him," she continued miserably, "then there's no sense in following the tour."

"But what about all that showbiz razzmatazz? The fans? The excitement?"

"It was great in the beginning. But the truth is, the fans only saw me as Mrs. Pedro Paloma, wife of the famous singer, and not as a real person in my own right. They want to know what Pedro eats, what he watches on TV, which side of the bed he sleeps on. Going on the road with him makes me feel like I'm invisible."

Winston watched helplessly as she wiped away a few tears that had escaped from her eyes. Wendy was one of his closest friends. He hated to see her miserable now. "That's tough," he murmured. "But you're talking about *divorce,* Wendy. That's *really* tough. Don't you still love Pedro?"

Wendy dropped her head and made an intense study of the bottom of her coffee cup.

"It's tea leaves that tell the future, not coffee dregs." Winston reached over and put his hand over hers.

Wendy looked up and smiled slightly. "Sorry, I'm stalling. It's just . . ." She trailed off, chewing on her bottom lip. "I don't know. I don't know what I think or what I feel anymore. That's half the problem. I feel so confused."

For the first time since their conversation started, Winston felt a little less helpless. He had the perfect idea. "We can find out, Wendy. We're in California, after all. There are a million

31

and one ways to get unconfused in this part of the country. You need to undertake a voyage of self-discovery and personal attunement."

Wendy's eyes grew wide, wider, until she burst out laughing. "Personal attunement?" she croaked. "I'm not a car!"

Winston found himself laughing too. Wendy's humor was infectious. "I know, I know." He chuckled. "But sometimes these things really help. I've seen it on *Oprah*."

"Oh, give me a break." Wendy groaned. "Could you see me on that show? 'I'm Wendy Paloma, and my marriage is falling apart. But my problem isn't another woman . . . it's a guitar!'"

Winston laughed harder and clutched at his torso. "Stop . . . you're making my ribs hurt."

Wendy took a sip of her orange juice, small giggles still escaping from her lips.

Pushing his glasses back up on his nose, Winston took a deep breath. "I'm serious, though. I think we should explore this. You have to figure out what's happening in your heart. And fast."

Wendy ducked her head, her slim shoulders rising before giving an involuntary shudder. "I know."

Nina felt as if she were lying on the bottom of the ocean. Everything seemed dark and murky. She couldn't focus. Her arms and legs felt leaden, but she knew she had to reach the surface before her air ran out.

Above her, miles away it seemed, she could make out a tiny speck of light. She was sure she could hear voices, her name even, being called over and over. But the sound was so faint, it was practically lost under the deep layers of water.

She struggled and kicked, but her limbs seemed wrapped in seaweed. *I must be drowning,* she thought hazily. But for the life of her she couldn't remember going into the water. *Don't the other lifeguards see me?*

Something shook her shoulder, and Nina felt herself being pulled gently upward. She tried to speak, but her mouth just opened and closed like a stranded fish's. The voices she'd heard were becoming clearer.

"Nina! Nina, are you all right?" Stu's anxious voice seemed to be coming from a great distance.

"Ohhh," she managed as she surfaced from the cloudy depths. She squinted at the light shining in her face. She expected to find herself washed ashore on the sandy beach. She blinked once at the familiar yellow walls. *But this is my room,* she thought. *How did I get to my room?*

Nina jerked herself up. "Ow," she complained, the sudden movement causing her head to pound. She looked around in confusion. "What happened?"

Stu stroked her hair, easing her throbbing head back into his lap. "Take it easy. You had a fall."

Nina frowned. "I was in the water. I thought I was drowning. How did I get here?"

Stu's handsome face was etched with concern. He gazed down at her and gently cradled her head. "We were going to check out the ocean," he told her. "But you were up here for such a long time, I got worried. When I came in, you were lying on the floor."

Nina frowned, trying to remember what had happened. "I must have fainted. Or maybe I hit my head on something." She struggled to get to her feet.

Stu propped her up with his muscular arms. "Have you eaten anything this morning?"

Nina started to shake her head but stopped halfway as the movement sent a shock wave of pain down to her toes. "I skipped breakfast."

Stu led her out of the room. "This is totally my fault. I shouldn't have woken you up so early and not fed you."

"That's not true." Nina smiled teasingly. "My spiritual food is much more important than any physical food."

"Not if the lack of it makes you faint," Stu replied anxiously. "You could have, like, really hurt yourself."

Nina rubbed the back of her head. She *did*

have a pretty big lump up there. She must have hit the floor full force. "Luckily I have a hard head," she said with a laugh.

"Come on," Stu offered, guiding her down the stairs. "I'll make you the Kirkwood special. The ultimate surfer's breakfast—eggs, home fries, breaded tomatoes . . ."

Nina pulled out the waistband of her peach sundress. "Now, hold on. I didn't diet all winter to gain everything back in one meal!"

Stu laughed. "You don't have to eat it all—just enough to keep you in one piece."

Nina slipped into a wooden chair at the kitchen table and watched contentedly while Stu puttered about the kitchen. *A killer bod and a whiz in the kitchen,* Nina thought happily. *I really have struck gold.*

They had just started tucking into their eggs when Nina was struck by a thought. She turned to Stu, her fork poised in midair with a big slice of pan-fried tomato impaled on it. "I know this is going to sound funny," she began cautiously, "but . . . but what was I doing up in my room?" Strangely, she couldn't remember.

Stu frowned and put down his fork. "You went up to change into your bathing suit."

Suddenly the white walls of the kitchen began to spin.

"Nina? Nina, are you OK?" Stu was at her

side in a second, his strong arm wrapped around her shoulders. "Maybe you should lie down. You look like you're going to faint again."

Nina leaped to her feet, ignoring the jolt of pain in her head. "I've got to show you something."

She ran out of the kitchen and up the stairs, taking the steps two at a time.

"Slow down, Nina," Stu called, running after her.

Nina burst into her bedroom and headed for her bed. "Where are they?" she cried. Her flowered bedspread was clear except for the usual pastel throw pillows.

Stu burst into the room, slightly out of breath. "What is it? You're totally freaking me out."

She turned on him, her dark brown eyes flashing. "Did you take them?"

"Take *what*? Calm down." He reached forward to pull her into his arms.

"My bathing suits!" she cried, pushing him away.

"Don't worry about the swim. We can go tomorrow."

Nina shook her head. "You don't understand. My bathing suits had been slashed to pieces, and I threw them onto my bed. They were right here." She pointed to the top of her bedspread. "They must have fallen behind it."

She crawled across her comforter to look down into the space between her headboard and the wall, wincing with pain as the blood rushed to the lump on her head.

Stu pulled her up and gently laid her on the bed. "You rest. I'll go look for your suits."

Nina lay propped up by the pillows as Stu made a thorough search of her bedroom. He found nothing.

"They must be here," Nina grumbled. "They were ripped to bits. I know I didn't put them away. My last memory was of throwing them onto the bed, right before . . ." She frowned. Was there something she wasn't remembering?

Stu ran a tanned hand across his forehead. "They're not here. Maybe they're on the clothesline outside. I'll check it out." He headed toward the stairs.

Nina closed her eyes, suddenly remembering how sure she'd been that someone else was in the room with her. "Don't bother, Stu," she whispered after him. "My suits are gone. And so is the person who tore them up."

The young woman watched, crouched in the tall grass behind the old Krebbs place. Stuart rushed out to the clothesline, where he pushed aside damp sheets, T-shirts, and towels.

"Nina's suits have to be here somewhere," she heard him mutter.

The left side of the young woman's face twitched in displeasure as she narrowed her almond-shaped eyes. "I have what you want, darling," she whispered, her voice masked by the ocean breeze. In her hands she twisted the tattered remains of Nina's bathing suits. "Nina can never love you like I do. She's a mere child."

The young woman winced as she remembered spying on Nina and Stuart kissing outside his beach house. Their tight embrace hadn't looked like child's play then. The young woman wound the suits even tighter between her hands, wringing them for all they were worth.

"What does Nina know about love anyway?" she hissed, staring at Stuart. "She might have tricked you into falling for her. But that can't keep us apart. We were meant to be together. It's fate. Nina's in the wrong place at the wrong time. An insignificant bug about to be squashed by our destiny."

The young woman watched as Stuart looked up at the window of her rival's room. *How can his face be full of tenderness?* she wondered. *Doesn't he see that Nina's love is a fake?*

"She's got nothing to offer him," the young woman muttered, kicking at the sand. "I can give him everything he'll ever need."

She cringed as she heard him speak. "My poor Nina," he said with a groan, still staring up at Nina's window. The young woman bit down hard on her lip as a howl struggled to escape from her mouth.

You're mine, she growled silently. *You're my soul mate.* She flung Nina's bathing suits to the ground, her mouth twisting into an angry grimace. "If only I'd had more time with her," she snarled. "Everything would be different now."

Stuart bent over the laundry basket and poked about inside, but soon stood empty-handed. The young woman made a low hissing sound, which made him turn toward where she was hiding in the grass. She flattened herself in the sand.

"Is anyone there?" he called, his forehead wrinkling into a frown.

A twisted smile spread across the young woman's face. "I'm here," she murmured softly. "Your true love." More than anything she wanted to stand up and let Stuart enfold her in his arms. But she knew it wasn't time yet. Not while Nina was still on the scene with her wily claws in him.

She flinched as Stuart angrily placed his hands on his narrow hips. "If anyone's out there, show yourself. I'm not into games."

"Don't be angry with me, Stuart," the young woman breathed. "She's the one playing with you. She must know you aren't meant to

39

be hers. It's you and I who are destined to be together. But I'll help you get over the spell she's put on you. I'll do whatever I must to make you mine."

She watched as Stuart grimaced and turned away. "Must be the wind," she heard him mutter as he started back toward the house.

The young woman groaned at the sight of his retreating back. It took all her self-control not to spring from the grass and wrap her yearning arms around him.

"Not yet," she told herself soothingly, rocking back and forth on her heels. "Not until I've gotten rid of Nina . . . permanently this time. Then Stuart will be mine again. Forever and ever and ever."

"Is that coffee for me?" Jessica asked. She climbed the last two steps up to the deck of the main lifeguard tower. Ryan was leaning casually over the wooden railing in a pair of khaki shorts and a blue T-shirt, staring out at the calm ocean.

He turned to her, a steaming mug in his hands, and lifted his dark sunglasses above his eyes. "Jessica." He smiled broadly. "What brings you out this early?"

"A beautiful day and the wonderful aroma of fresh-brewed coffee?" Jessica offered. She tentatively shrugged her tanned shoulders and adjusted her white halter top. She would never admit that Ben's snide comments had driven her out of the house a good hour before she needed to report for lifeguard duty.

Ryan threw back his head and laughed. His teeth were a gleaming white against his suntanned face. "If I'd known beautiful women were so easily attracted by coffee, I would have started my percolator last night."

Jessica smiled in confusion and brushed back her long, golden blond hair. *What an un-Ryan-like thing to say,* she thought. "Well, I'm here now," she stated. "And I sure could use a sip." She reached out for Ryan's mug.

"Not so fast." He chuckled, taking a small step backward. "There's plenty in the pot."

"Ryan," she persisted, "I just want a sip." She reached forward. But as quick as a wink Ryan jumped back, holding the coffee mug securely behind him.

"I know your type." He grinned. "You say a sip but take a gulp."

Reaching around his waist, Jessica tried to grab for the mug. "Don't be silly," she said with a giggle. "Now give me that coffee!"

"Sorry, Jess. Nothing doing!" Then to Jessica's total surprise, Ryan leaped up onto the thin wooden railing encircling the deck.

"Ryan," she cried. "What's gotten into you?"

41

Clowning around was the last thing she expected from Ryan. He wasn't exactly Mr. Spontaneous. In fact, Mr. Uptight-serious-guy was more like it. "You'd better give me that mug before you fall and break it."

Ryan balanced precariously on one leg. "Not on your life, dear girl!" he shouted in a silly English accent. He tottered back and forth along the railing. "I always wanted to do this," he shouted, balancing the coffee mug on his head. "Whooo! No hands!"

Jessica watched in utter amazement as he continued to stroll along the banister. Was this the same head lifeguard who'd strictly forbidden any goofing around at the main tower or the posts? He was acting as if aliens had come down in the night and replaced him. *Either that or that's some very powerful coffee,* she thought.

Ryan jumped down in front of her and smiled sheepishly. "Ta-da."

Jessica crossed her slender arms over her chest in mock seriousness. "*Now* can I have my sip of coffee?"

Ryan smiled as he flung the mug's contents over his shoulder. "Sorry, Jess, all gone. But I'll tell you what—as a consolation prize, I hereby offer you a free dance around our spacious lifeguard deck." In a flash he grabbed Jessica's hands and started to do a quick two-step, expertly dipping her so low, her head nearly hit the wooden plank floor.

"Ryan!" she gasped, laughing. "What's gotten into you?"

Ryan righted her and shrugged his broad shoulders. "I've had enough of this being-serious business. It's time for me to relax."

Jessica nodded as she tugged her red miniskirt back into position. She couldn't agree more—where most things were concerned. "But not while you're lifeguarding, of course."

"Of course," Ryan agreed amicably. "That wouldn't be good at all. But for everything else—live and let live is my new motto."

Jessica nodded again. *I couldn't have put it better myself,* she thought. Lately it seemed as if everyone—Elizabeth, Ben, and especially Priya—was just a little too serious for her taste.

Ryan ran a hand through his wavy, sun-streaked hair and gave her a sly smile. "I could take some lessons from you, Jessica. Having fun has always been your priority, hasn't it?"

Jessica felt a self-conscious shiver pass through her as Ryan's gold-flecked brown eyes bore into hers. "Yes," she agreed in a near whisper. Why was Ryan looking at her like that? *Is he flirting with me?* she thought suddenly. *No way, right?* He was her sister's boyfriend, after all!

A broad smile spread across his lips as he

leaned against the railing and crossed his arms, showing off his biceps to perfection. "Then you and I are in perfect agreement, wouldn't you say?"

Jessica gulped and dropped her eyes. She'd almost forgotten the enormous crush she'd had on Ryan the previous summer. Now it was all coming back to her—his gorgeous body rippling with muscles; the way his handsome, tanned face could break into a bright smile when she'd done a particularly skillful lifeguard maneuver. But last year, despite her attempts to attract him, that was as far as it had gone. Ryan had been uptight and serious; it had made perfect sense when he'd hooked up with Elizabeth.

Jessica looked back into Ryan's eyes. "I guess so," she offered uncertainly.

"Guess so?" Ryan teased. "I *know* so."

Jessica gulped again. *What's going on here?* she wondered, her head spinning. Ryan's sexy gaze was locked on to hers like a heat-seeking missile. She tried to squelch the feelings of attraction, but her temperature was definitely rising. After all, Ryan *was* six-foot four inches of pure, oceangoing, muscular male. And he *was* flirting with her!

But he's also *your sister's boyfriend,* Jessica reminded herself firmly.

She gritted her teeth and tore her eyes away from Ryan's. *Where is Liz?* she thought. She suddenly realized she hadn't seen her twin sister or their cherry red Jeep all morning. She looked back at Ryan. "Have you seen Elizabeth?" she asked. "Do you know where she is?"

Ryan suddenly turned to gaze out at the ocean. "I'm not your sister's keeper," he growled.

Jessica frowned. "I just thought if there was a problem—"

Ryan turned back to her, the sexy grin back on his face. "Problem?" He shrugged again. "What problem could there be when the lovely Jessica Wakefield is around?"

Ryan, I don't know what's gotten into you, Jessica said silently, *but I wish you'd stop flashing those drop-dead gorgeous eyes at me.* Ryan Taylor had been the source of enough confusion between her and Elizabeth the previous summer. There was no way she wanted a repeat this year. The last thing she wanted was more trouble.

There you are, Ryan, Elizabeth thought with relief as she hurried toward the main lifeguard tower. She could see him leaning against the railing, sharing what looked like a good laugh with her twin sister.

"Things can't be that bad," she murmured. "Ryan certainly looks like he's in a good mood."

But why didn't he take my calls? she wondered with a twinge of uneasiness.

She walked quickly up the wooden walkway, feeling sweaty and slightly out of breath. Her once-crisp white dress hung on her slender body like seaweed. Her taxi had become hopelessly ensnared in beachgoing traffic, so she'd decided to abandon it and half walk, half run the last mile. She'd been desperate to get to the beach before her shift started so she could track down Ryan and put last night's misunderstanding behind them.

"Hi," she called with forced brightness as she reached the bottom of the steps. Both Ryan and Jessica looked down, suddenly falling silent, their happy smiles disappearing from view. She felt like a dark cloud that had just passed over their sunshine. "Is something the matter?"

Ryan shrugged. "What could be the matter?" He turned back to Jessica. "You were saying?"

Elizabeth frowned at his chilly reception. *Is Ryan deliberately freezing me out?* she thought, flinching.

Jessica gave a nervous laugh and tugged at the bottom of her red miniskirt. "Nothing important."

Elizabeth narrowed her sea green eyes as she looked from her sister to her boyfriend. She couldn't shake off the uncomfortable feeling that she'd walked in on something. "Jess, isn't your shift about to start?"

"No sooner than yours," Ryan cut in.

Elizabeth cleared her throat and gave her twin a warning look.

Jessica made a face as if to say, *I'm on my way,* and then took a step toward the stairs. "I'd better straighten up my floats."

"I can help you with that," Ryan offered, starting after her.

Elizabeth stepped in front of him. "Ryan!"

Ryan scowled. "I'll come by later, Jess. I think your sister wants to speak to me."

Jessica shrugged as she bounded down the stairs. "Later, guys."

Elizabeth watched until Jessica was out of earshot and then turned to her boyfriend. "Ryan, I want to explain about last night. Did you get my messages?"

Ryan held up his hand. "Forget about it." He turned and started inside the main lifeguard tower.

"But how can you say that?" Elizabeth called, following after him. "I can see you're upset with me. I want you to understand what happened."

He flopped down into his red leather captain's chair and began to study the weave of his khaki shorts. "I do understand, and I really couldn't care less."

"Ryan," Elizabeth said gravely, her stomach lurching. "You obviously *don't* understand, or you wouldn't be acting like this."

Ryan gave her a withering look. "Since when are you an expert on human psychology? I'm tired, OK? I didn't have a very good time last night. All alone. No date."

Elizabeth closed her eyes and rocked back on her heels. "I know. But it's not my fault. I had trouble with the Jeep. I just came from the garage."

"Yeah, I got that impression from the ten messages you left. So I know it's not *your* fault. Which I guess means it's *my* fault, is that right?" Ryan indignantly pointed a finger at his own chest. "You were too busy to drive to the restaurant with *me* last night. But I guess that's my fault too."

"Ryan, please—"

"Let's see." Ryan narrowed his eyes crossly. "Is there anything else that's my fault? How about my wanting to treat you to the finest seafood in southern California? Yep, I'm to blame for that too. I actually *deigned* to interrupt your busy schedule. I even had the nerve, as I waited in that restaurant, to think I'd *at least* get a phone call from you." He laced his fingers behind his head and glared at her for a moment before looking away. "Don't worry. I won't make those mistakes again."

Elizabeth took a deep breath and tried to keep her hands from shaking. *What's gotten into him?* she wondered. *Ryan's being totally unreasonable. In fact, he's making no sense at all. I knew he'd be upset, but this is ridiculous.*

"Ryan, *please,*" she implored. "I'm trying to explain. I couldn't call you at the restaurant because I was stranded on the highway. Why won't you listen to me?"

Ryan refused to catch her eye. He rubbed his hands compulsively up and down the armrest of his captain's chair before pushing himself to his feet. "I'm a little under the weather, I guess. Must be a summer cold." He took a step toward her.

Elizabeth felt her body relax. *It's OK,* she thought. *He's going to kiss me.* She closed her eyes as his body leaned closer. In a moment she would be in his arms. She could almost feel the pressure of his warm skin against hers. The salty taste of the sea on his sensuous lips. He understood. They would celebrate another time.

But instead of being pulled against his chest, Elizabeth felt Ryan's arm brush past her. She snapped open her eyes to see he was holding the handle to the door.

"Do you mind?" he said.

Elizabeth's mouth dropped open. It wasn't a question at all—Ryan was ushering her out! Stunned, she took a step back and found herself staring into the main lifeguard tower from the porch.

"But Ryan!" she cried. "We haven't worked this out!"

He shrugged. "Some other time," he mumbled, letting the screen door swing shut in her face.

Elizabeth gasped, tears welling in her eyes as the sound of a bolt being pushed into place resounded with shuddering finality.

Chapter Three

"Wake up, sleepyhead," Stu murmured, his arm draped loosely around Nina's bare shoulders. "We're almost there."

Nina stirred, stretching her slender arms and smoothing down the skirt of her peach sundress. She gazed drowsily over the side of Stu's wooden rowboat and dipped one hand in the cool blue water. The warm glow of the sun was reflected in the gently lapping waves. "Where are we going?"

Stu laughed and kissed her forehead. "You'll see. I don't want to ruin the surprise." He leaned forward and took hold of the oars.

Nina watched in admiration as Stu's powerful arms flexed beneath the thin material of his T-shirt with each careful and deliberate stroke through the water. She really had no idea where they were *or* where they were heading. The lazy drift through the inlet had worked wonders on her nerves after the incident at the beach house, but she wasn't sure a surprise was the best thing for her right now. She hoped that whatever was coming next wouldn't undo her serenity.

Nina reached for her bottle of moisturizer and rubbed some on her soft, dusky legs. "How about a hint?"

Stu grinned broadly and made the zipped-lips sign. He maneuvered the rowboat through a tall clump of weeds, jumping out and looping the mooring line around an outcropping of rock. "Just a second."

"A second?" Nina took his outstretched hand and stepped out of the boat beside him. Before them stood a large, ramshackle beach house painted in coral pink and lime. "There? Is that where we're going?"

"Getting warm."

Nina stopped and placed her hands on her hips. "Tell me, or I'm not taking one more step."

Stu's mouth twisted into a lopsided grin. "OK, one clue. I'm taking my shoes off." He pulled off his tattered boating sneakers.

Nina made a face. "What kind of clue is that? You always go around barefoot."

Stu grinned. "But this is special. Come on, take off your shoes."

Nina leaned against him and removed her peach-colored lace-up sandals. "Now what's this surprise?" she asked, slinging them over her back.

Stu led her around the side of the house to a secluded area framed on one side by high sand dunes and wild salt grass. She could see a group of about twenty people gathered closely on the beach. She didn't recognize anyone.

"What is it?" she whispered, burning with curiosity. She could hear low chanting and soft clapping, and as she and Stu approached, Nina began to feel an awesome surge of energy coming from the group. Stu ushered her to the front of the circle.

"Wow," Nina gasped. At the center of the group was a long bed—maybe twelve feet—of hot coals. At one end of the coals an older man with a magnificent white beard and a woman dressed in a colorful sarong were huddled in intense conversation. Suddenly, to Nina's amazement, the woman in the sarong stepped up onto the coals and began serenely walking across them *with no shoes on*. Fire walking!

Nina gulped, her dark eyes doubling in size. Stu had told her that people, if they channeled their mental powers, could walk on hot coals without suffering any serious injury. He'd even showed her the proper breathing techniques and state-of-mind exercises. But she hadn't realized people actually *did* it!

The woman completed the fire walk and jumped into a large pan of water that had been set up at the opposite end of the coals.

"Feel the power," the crowd chanted. "Feel the power."

"It's a radical feeling," Stu whispered, bending his head close to hers. "Mind over matter, knowing you're in control of your own body and what can affect it."

"I'm sure, but talking and doing are two different things . . . ," Nina began as Stu moved to the head of the bed of coals and nodded to the elderly bearded man. "Guru Cosi Momo," she heard Stu say. She watched with growing incredulousness as Stu took a few deep breaths. To the group's delight—and Nina's horror—he stepped onto the bed of glowing embers.

"Stu!" Nina screamed, reaching out for him, terrified he'd burn himself. But he was already gone, skating across the hot coals as if they were ice. He turned once at the middle and winked at her before completing the rest of his walk, stepping quickly into the large pan of water.

"Feel the power." The crowd's chanting was punctuated with shouts and murmurs of approval. Nina remained silent, gaping at Stu in utter shock.

Stu waved to her from the far end. Her jaw dropped when all eyes turned toward her and the low chanting began to grow louder. Stu was gesturing for *her* to follow him across!

"Oh, my gosh!" Wendy gasped. "Winston, come quick! It's Nina!"

Winston squeezed between two women in gauzy, ankle-length dresses to meet Wendy at the edge of the smoldering coals. He and Wendy had been strolling along the beach, hoping for a beautiful sunset, when they'd spotted the smoke from the dunes. After they'd come closer to investigate, Winston couldn't believe his eyes when he saw a surfer guy walking across burning coals—in his bare feet no less!

"Nina!" he cried over the low chanting of the crowd, waving his hand to catch her eye. *Nina Harper? Walk across hot coals?* he marveled. *No way. It'll never happen.* The guy in the baggy Bermuda shorts had made it look easy. And maybe under the right kind of hypnosis—or was it *psychosis*—it was easy. But Nina? It didn't seem possible.

Nina caught Winston's eye and jumped as if startled. She waved and hurried over.

Wendy's gray eyes were as wide as saucers. "This is so cool!" she squealed, turning to Nina.

"*Hot,* not cool." Winston fanned his face. "How do they do that?"

"I don't know," Nina exclaimed, grabbing

onto Winston's Hawaiian shirt and ducking behind him. "But you got here in the nick of time!"

"Nina," Winston said with a laugh. "I didn't know you were a fire walker."

"Are you really going to do it?" Wendy asked in amazement.

"I'm not!" she cried, nervously twisting the hem of her dress. "I'm here with . . . um . . . a friend of mine. He showed me the deep-breathing exercises, but I'm terrified."

Winston raised one eyebrow. *"He?"*

Two red spots appeared on Nina's cheeks, and she quickly ducked her head as the tall, muscular guy in the baggy shorts loped toward them. "Um . . . Winston, Wendy, this is my friend Stu," she mumbled. "Stu, Winston and Wendy."

Friend, huh? Winston thought as he watched Nina's blush spread across her face. He hadn't forgotten the big point Nina had made of swearing off guys for the summer. Maybe fire walkers didn't count. He suppressed a giggle.

Stu nodded a greeting; the curls in his shoulder-length, white-blond hair bobbed up and down. "Awesome experience, man. You ought to try it."

"Are deep-breathing exercises all it takes?" Wendy asked.

Winston whipped his head around to stare at his friend. "You can't be serious!"

"Really!" Nina added. "You could get hurt doing that if you're not prepared for it."

Winston didn't like the mischievous look on Wendy's face one bit. "Not unless you're wearing ten-inch platform heels," Winston added, pointing at the red-hot coals vigorously. "But judging by the length of that walk, even *they* might burn through."

Stu shook his head. "Don't worry, Winston. Fire walking is all about state of mind. If you let your skeptical, fearful parts rule you, then six-foot-high stilts will burn through. But if you allow yourself to step through the membrane of fear, you won't get burned at all. What do you say, guys? Who's going to go first?"

Winston shook his head and shoved his hands into the pockets of his khakis. He liked his barbecues the old-fashioned way—with him being the chef, not the main course.

Nina pointed a trembling finger at Wendy. "You can have the honors."

Winston watched the conflicting emotions running across Wendy's face. The two robed women next to them nodded their encouragement. "It's a once-in-a-lifetime experience," the older woman said, her large silver earrings tinkling.

Suddenly Stu called over a tall, bearded man in a turquoise robe. "This is Guru Cosi Momo," Stu said. "He's a fire-walking master. Wendy, he can show you the proper breathing exercises."

Wendy and Winston exchanged glances. "Should I?" Wendy whispered eagerly. "You said I should undertake a voyage of self-discovery and personal attunement."

Winston winced. *Next time I'll keep my big mouth shut,* he thought. *I wanted Wendy to search her soul, not scorch her sole!* He looked pleadingly at Wendy, but the excited sparkle in her gray eyes told him he'd been beat. "OK." He sighed. "Go for it."

Wendy squealed and gave him a big hug. The two women nodded sagely. "Show me what to do," Wendy cried, kicking off her leather sandals. "And let me at 'em."

Winston ran to the other end of the bed of hot embers to wait for her. "Go, Wendy!" he called, crossing his fingers as Guru Cosi Momo bent his head and spoke quietly to her. Wendy nodded and then took a few deep breaths, locking eyes with Winston's through the shimmering heat waves rising from the coals. "Feel the power," he shouted, echoing the chant of the other spectators.

Winston watched in awe as Wendy took off, tearing across the burning bed, an astonished smile plastered across her face. She let out a loud "Yeah!" as she jumped into the pan of water at the end of the walk. The group cheered their support. "Well done!" the woman with the tinkling earrings called out.

"It didn't hurt at all," Wendy gushed as she leaped out of the water pan and dove into Winston's arms. "I wish Pedro had been here to see me to do that!"

"He would have been blown away," Winston agreed, gleefully spinning her around. But when he stopped and let her go, he realized she was no longer smiling. "What's wrong?"

Wendy drew a line in the sand with her toe. "But Pedro's not." She shook her head sadly. "Not here." She indicated the vibrant group surrounding the hot coals. "Or in here." She laid a hand against the front of her striped sundress to indicate her heart.

Winston pulled her hand away. "That's not true. Pedro was the first person you mentioned when you came off the coals. And after an emotionally charged experience, that's really important. It proves you still love him."

"No," Wendy insisted to Winston's dismay. She bent down to pick up her sandals. "It means I'm working Pedro out of my system. And the sooner that's done, the better."

"Feel the power," the young woman chanted at the back of the fire-walking crowd. She tugged on the brim of her big, floppy hat to cover her face. *I'm taking a big risk being out here*, she thought, shifting uneasily. *Someone might recognize me.*

All she needed was one curious spectator looking a little too long and her cover would be blown. The notion made her heart pound and her palms turn sweaty. She wiped them along her dress and took a deep breath. *I've come too far now*, she thought. *I've got to keep my cool.*

"Anyway," she assured herself under her breath, "in this disguise, I look like all the other New Age wackos." She looked down at the baggy purple housedress, which was swimming on her tall, lanky frame.

The young woman chuckled as she remembered how shocked the cashier at the used clothing store looked when she'd traded in one of her usual pairs of skintight jeans for this dowdy outfit. But her usual clothes attracted too much attention; until she'd taken care of Nina Harper, attracting attention would *not* be a good idea.

She surveyed the scene from behind her oversize sunglasses. *What a designer's nightmare*, she thought. Underfed men with straggly beards and tie-dyed T-shirts; spaced-out women in shapeless muumuus. *I feel like I'm at a retro hippie convention.*

She wove her way farther into the group to

get closer to the center. Stuart had moved out of her range of vision to the other side of the long bed of hot coals. *Not being with him from day to day is bad enough,* she thought. *But now that we're this close, not being able to see him is like an itch I've got to scratch.* "No matter how dangerous it is," she murmured, coming up to the edge of the bed of coals.

"Feel the power!" the young woman called out again, aping the rest of the crowd as they cheered on none other than Wendy Wolman—wait, Wendy Wolman *Paloma*. She'd had run-ins with that plain Jane before. "How's your hubby, Pedro?" the young woman whispered menacingly. "You're lucky I only have eyes for my Stuart, or I'd lead your little man astray just for spite."

The young woman turned her eyes away from Wendy and back to the place where she'd last seen Stuart. She gasped. Stuart was gone, replaced by a straggly haired New Ager! She jumped back to gain higher ground in the sand dunes. If she lost Stuart now, she wasn't sure how long it would take her to catch up with him again. Following him and Nina as they'd drifted along in his rowboat—that had been a nightmare. She had scratches and bruises all down her legs and arms from crashing through the underbrush along the shore. No, she hadn't gone through all that for nothing.

She elbowed her way past two men in quiet conversation to climb to the top of the dune.

"Go in peace," one of the men advised.

The young woman snarled. "Save your mumbo jumbo for the other cranks," she growled, but bit her lip. She couldn't afford any confrontations now.

The group around the bed of hot coals began another low chant of "feel the power." Her eyes searched frantically until they locked on to Stu's familiar sun-streaked head. He was standing with Nina and that freakish guru. "That can only mean one thing," she murmured. "Nina's getting ready to take a little walk."

The young woman snorted in disgust. Even from her position in the dunes she could sense the group's zombielike support for Nina. She shook her head bitterly. Pretending to support Wendy was one thing, but there was no way she could yell out encouragement for Nina unless it was, *Burn, witch, burn!*

She giggled as a lightbulb went on in her head. *Nina will be wide open and vulnerable now,* she realized with an evil smile. She headed quickly down the dune and slipped back into the group, stealthily positioning herself at the far end of the bed of coals between two women in large white turbans.

"Stuart won't be the only thing waiting for

Nina when she steps out of that pan of water."
The young woman snickered to herself. "I'll be
here to give her an experience she'll never forget."

"Come on, Nina," Stu cried, clasping her
hand. "Don't back out now. You've got to try it."

"Definitely," Wendy piped up. "I've never
felt more alive."

"But what if I get burned!" Nina cried, pointing to the glowing coals that stretched before her
menacingly. "These are the only feet I have."

Wendy laughed. "Stu has already taught you
the breathing techniques, and Guru Cosi Momo
has showed you how to center yourself. It's easy
as long as you concentrate."

Stu nodded. "Guru Cosi Momo wouldn't
have given you the OK if he didn't think you
could handle it."

Nina sighed hesitantly, looking from Stu to
Wendy. Both their faces were electrified. And
each had described walking across the hot coals
as one of their most exhilarating experiences.
But what if I somehow get it wrong? she worried.

Nina shoved her hands into the pockets of
her sundress. She'd never felt more agitated or
uncertain. Should she or shouldn't she? She
kicked at a seashell with her bare toe. The hot
coals lay spread out before her on the sand, their
centers glowing brightly in brilliant oranges and

fiery reds. She felt excited, scared, and anxious all at the same time.

What should I do? she wondered. It seemed as if every person in the crowd was watching her expectantly.

"Don't worry, dear," an elderly woman in a hot pink sari assured her. "You can do it. I was seventy-two the first time I did."

Nina smiled. "Thanks for the support, but—"

"Now, no buts," the older woman playfully scolded. "You listen to your friends." She turned away and went back to chanting.

Nina gripped the sleeve of Stu's T-shirt. "You and Wendy made it look so simple. What if I trip or suddenly forget what I'm doing and freeze?"

Stu pulled her close. "Don't be afraid," he murmured tenderly into her hair. "Trust me, you'll be fine."

Nina looked down at her feet and squeezed the sand with her toes. *Trust,* she echoed silently. *That old concept again. Not an easy thing to do after your long-term boyfriend has betrayed you.* But then her heart reminded her that this was Stu who was talking. He'd done nothing to hurt her. All he'd done was be the truest and most loving man she'd ever met.

Nina looked again at the glowing faces surrounding the bed of hot coals. Each person was smiling at her with encouragement. Everyone here believed in her. Wendy and Winston believed in her. Even the guru of fire walking, Cosi Momo, believed in her.

Why can't I trust them back? she asked herself.

Nina took a deep breath. She knew that if she refused, Stu would be fine. He was only gently coaxing her, not daring her. Still, she was never one to back down from a challenge. With his support she hoped—*trusted*—she could do it. "OK," she agreed. "I'll do the walk."

The crowd clapped and their chanting grew more spirited. "Feel the power. Feel the power."

Stu ran to the other end of the bed of coals. He held out his arms, a welcoming grin stretched across his face.

Nina stepped up to the burning embers. She took a deep breath and let it out slowly. *Feel the power,* she thought as she shook her head and rolled her shoulders. And then, as Guru Cosi Momo had instructed her, she channeled all her thoughts to one image. That image was of Stu, helping her to unlock a door, behind which were the powerful feelings she held for him in her heart.

She took one more deep breath and all of a sudden the door flew open, setting free a surge of beautiful, loving emotions that surrounded her with protective energy. Without thinking or doubting a moment more, Nina stepped out onto the coals and began to walk.

Time seemed to slow down. Nina felt as if she were floating on a cloud, her legs moving effortlessly. Instead of experiencing a searing pain as her bare feet moved across the burning coals, she felt a sheltering warmth that seemed to surround her and carry her along. *I feel the power,* she thought as the problems of the temporal world dropped away.

As Nina's feet hit the water at the other end of the coal bed she fell into Stu's delighted arms, nearly overcome by the most intense swell of emotional connection and personal fulfillment she'd ever experienced. Stu turned her to face the group. They called out their support and congratulations. A powerful wave of love and trust welled up within her. "I can't ever remember feeling this connected and happy," she gushed, her arms spread out to take it all in.

Suddenly a section of the bed of coals flared up, creating a stir in the group. As Nina spun around to see what had caused it, she felt a sharp shove squarely on her back. Off-balance, she felt herself pitching forward. A terrified scream was strangled in her throat as she began plummeting downward—face first toward the scorching coals!

Chapter Four

"Now what am I going to do?" Jessica muttered, twisting the last bit of water out of her long blond hair and clipping it up at the back of her head inside the lifeguard changing room. "I can't bear to go home!"

The prospect of facing Ben—and possibly Priya—now that her shift was over was positively revolting. She'd been fuming off and on the whole day, and she still hadn't come up with a way to get Ben back!

"That's because you don't know whether you want to hurt him as your sworn enemy or to win him over as your boyfriend," she chided herself under her breath.

Jessica rolled her aquamarine eyes as she pulled an oversize white button-down shirt from her bag and slipped it on over her halter top. It was still hard for her to believe Ben wasn't somehow punishing her for not calling and writing to him over the school year. After all, she had promised him her undying love when they'd parted last summer.

But it's not my fault we fell out of touch, Jessica thought, shrugging as she pulled on her red miniskirt. *I've always been the out-of-sight, out-of-mind type. I'll make it up to him. Now that he's back in my sights, he's firmly in my mind.*

"Hey, Jess," Miranda Reese called, pushing through the doors into the changing room. "Now that our shift's over, want to go shopping?"

"Great idea!" Jessica enthused, tying the long ends of her shirt around her waist. Shopping would keep her out of the beach house—and away from Ben. "But I thought you were on a budget," she said, looking over at Miranda's chinos and tight black T-shirt. "Didn't you buy that outfit yesterday?"

The edges of Miranda's mouth turned down and she sighed. "I know, but it's either go shopping or go back to the beach house. And with Miss Know-it-all Priya Rahman there, I'd rather go into hock."

"You too?" Jessica groaned. "Ben ran me out of the house first thing this morning. What a way to start the day. One more snide remark from him and I'm going to scream."

"Tell me about it!" Miranda cried. "I can't even boil an egg without her insisting she knows how to do it better."

Miranda ran her fingers through her long brown hair and gave a little toss of her head in a perfect imitation of Priya. "You realize, of course, Miranda," she mimicked, "if you put salt in the water after you start the boil, you'll get a more even bubble."

Jessica laughed. "All I can say is that it's a good thing there were no six-foot-tall, tanned guys in U of C baseball caps struggling in the water today or I might have looked the other way."

Miranda shook her head. "Between the two of them we're going to end up sleeping on the street!"

Jessica smirked. "Can't you see them standing over us? 'That's not the proper way to sleep on a park bench. You must have your feet pointing *south*.'"

Miranda snickered, shaking her head. "Unfortunately, yes. I *can* see it all too well. So how about it? I hear Mermaids is having a sale on bathing suits."

Jessica rolled her damp red lifeguard suit in her towel and shoved it into her bag. "You don't have to twist my arm. The way I feel about Ben and Priya, I'd show up for a sale at the hardware store." She headed out for the boardwalk with Miranda following her.

"Hey!" Miranda exclaimed, stopping in her tracks on the busy esplanade. "Hardware store? That's not a bad idea. Cute guys are always buying tools."

Jessica groaned playfully and reached out to pull her friend by the arm. "First we get the new bathing suits, then we can show up at the hardware store. And anyway, Mermaids is in this direction."

Miranda grinned and linked arms with Jessica as they started walking again. A few minutes later they were in front of Mermaids, the first of a strip of exclusive shops lining the far side of the boardwalk. It was a small, tastefully furnished boutique. Four sales racks full of swimsuits stood in the middle of the store. Jessica and Miranda headed for the size-six section, happy to see there was a good selection left.

"Ohhh," Jessica breathed, "this is gorgeous." She pulled a shimmering aquamarine one-piece from the rack. It was cut high at the legs and low at the neckline.

"It sure is," Miranda declared. "And the color is an exact match for your eyes."

Jessica ran to the mirror and held up the suit against her white shirt and red miniskirt. *Miranda's right,* she thought. The sexy one-piece was making her eyes sparkle like sapphires.

"I would love to see Ben's face if I sashayed into the kitchen in this little number," she murmured, remembering his earlier insult about her skirt looking too tight. "This would knock that smirk off his face."

Miranda came up behind her, her arms laden down with bathing suits. "You should get it," she said encouragingly. "Priya has the same one, but I'm sure you'll look a million times better."

Jessica cringed and looked at the suit again. Suddenly her fantasy turned sour as she imagined Priya slinking into the kitchen next to her. She looked slim and gorgeous while Jessica blew up four sizes, splitting the seams of the bathing suit in two. She imagined herself waddling from the room while Ben and Priya laughed at her like hyenas.

Jessica shook her head angrily and tossed the suit back onto the rack. "I don't think so," she pouted. "I'm sick of being compared to Priya." She blindly grabbed a bunch of bathing suits and marched off in the direction of the changing rooms.

"Ready?" Miranda called a few moments later.

"Ready," Jessica replied, stifling a giggle.

Both girls flung open their changing-room doors. Miranda popped out in a dynamite, powder blue string bikini; Jessica posed dramatically in a baggy, old-ladies'-style skirted one-piece in a vile, pasty beige.

71

Miranda practically dropped to the floor in laughter. "That's so *you,* Gramma Wakefield, but your knees are showing!"

"My word," Jessica quipped. "How risqué of me."

"Wow!"

Jessica and Miranda whipped around to discover the source of the unfamiliar, deep male voice. A gorgeous dark-haired, blue-eyed guy with a deep tan stood before them, scuba-diving equipment slipping out of his arms. He was staring at Miranda.

Miranda smiled. "You like my suit?" she asked, doing a slow turn.

The guy gulped. "I sure do." He dropped to the floor to retrieve the gear, all the time staring at her. "I'm Jamie, the store manager. What a knockout—" he started. "I mean, the bathing suit, of course." He blushed crimson. "Hey," he said suddenly, "we're having a fashion show next week and need two more girls. Do you think you could be one of our models?"

Jessica's ears perked up excitedly. A fashion show would be the perfect thing to win Ben back! "I'm available," she announced.

The store manager looked at her and blinked. "Um, sorry, ma'am," he stuttered, looking totally appalled. "But, uh, those positions are all filled."

"What do you mean?" Jessica asked. "You just said there were *two* positions."

"Um . . . yes, but . . . ," the store manager stammered.

Jessica threw her hands to her hips. "So? What's the problem?"

The store manager pulled at the collar of his polo shirt. "You . . . um . . . don't quite fit the profile we're looking for."

"Profile?" Jessica demanded. "What profile? Beautiful blondes aren't good enough?"

"Er . . ."

Jessica's mouth dropped open as the store manager's hesitation hit her full force. He *thinks* I'm *plain?* she wondered in shock. *How* could *he?*

She turned on her heels and ran back to the changing room, rushing to the mirror. Tears of humiliation came to her eyes when she saw herself in the baggy granny suit. She had completely forgotten she had it on. "Some funny joke," Jessica whined. "The joke's on *me.* No wonder he didn't want me to model!"

Still, he should have been able to see past the stupid swimsuit, she thought, sniffling. *First Ben scorns me, and now totally hunky guys aren't even noticing I exist. Have I lost the old Wakefield magic?*

*   *   *

73

"Help!" Nina screamed. The huge bed of burning coals seemed to be rushing toward her terrified eyes in nightmarish slow motion. She felt her mind blanking out as it prepared for the searing agony that was sure to come. *No!* she thought desperately. *Not this. Anything but this!*

With only milliseconds to spare she felt Stu's strong arms yank her flailing body back toward him. She spun, falling into the sand right beside the bed of flaming embers—close enough to feel the heat of the coals on her face. The group of fire walkers gasped.

Stu was down at her side in a flash, holding her close. As her terror subsided, her tears took over, streaming freely as Stu helped her uncertainly to her feet.

"Please take me home," Nina sobbed, clinging to him for dear life. "I want to get out of here." Her arm ached where Stu had grabbed it, and her cry of help was ricocheting in her head.

"Who could do such a thing?" the woman in the hot pink sari cried.

Nina buried her face in Stu's T-shirt. *One of you,* she thought with horror, peeking out at the group of people surrounding them. She couldn't bare to make eye contact with anyone. Moments before they'd been her friends; now each one was a potential enemy. She brushed away her tears as she leaned heavily against Stu.

"Did anyone see who pushed her?" Stu demanded.

The women in the white turbans shook their heads.

"I didn't see anything," the woman with the tinkling earrings responded.

"Or me," added one of the men in the tie-dyed T-shirts. "I guess we were all too busy looking at the coal flare-up."

Stu hugged Nina tightly against him. "I'm sorry, little mermaid," he whispered, stroking her forehead.

"Nina! Nina, are you all right?" Winston called, pushing through the fire walkers who had surrounded her. He grabbed hold of her hand as Wendy came alongside them, her face pale and upset.

"I'm OK," Nina said wearily. "Just . . . upset . . ." She took a deep breath before fresh tears could start.

Winston sighed with relief, but his face was still full of concern. "Wendy and I will take you home right away."

Nina shook her head. "Stu's taking me home," she murmured. She watched as Winston and Wendy exchanged glances. Nina closed her eyes. She didn't have the energy to deny what they obviously realized by now.

"Please, guys." She leaned forward and

75

whispered so Stu couldn't hear. "Do me a favor and don't—"

"Don't tell anyone about you and Stu?" Winston guessed quietly. "Hey, your secret's safe with us. After all that fuss you made about your no-guys pledge this summer, I can understand why you'd want to keep this under wraps."

"It's not like that," Nina insisted. "Not exactly. Stu is really special."

"I understand," Wendy said softly.

Winston nodded solemnly. "If there's anything we can do . . ."

Nina clung harder to Stu. "Thanks, you two." But she knew she wouldn't feel all right until she was far away. "Please, Stu," she said, swallowing a sob. "Take me home now."

Stu held her close as he led her through the crowd, one protective arm wrapped around her shoulders. Nina kept her eyes tightly shut, stumbling once or twice on the uneven rising of the sand dunes. But she preferred her self-imposed blindness to the sympathetic faces that might have been hiding an attacker.

"We're almost to the rowboat," Stu whispered.

Nina opened her eyes, sore from the sparks of the coals and her own hot tears. They were near the bank of the inlet, far away from the crowd.

"Who would do such a thing?" Nina moaned.

"A totally deranged mind," Stu responded.

Nina shuddered. Was it all a bizarre coincidence? Or had she already encountered that deranged mind before?

Winston pointed excitedly at the gorgeous array of bright, twinkling stars filling up the evening sky. "Did you see that one, Elizabeth?" he asked her.

Elizabeth shifted her position on the stairs to the back porch of the Krebbs' beach house. She giggled and shook her head, pulling up the hood of her white SVU sweatshirt as protection against the cool night air. "I think you're making it up, Winston. What's that, the third shooting star you've seen?"

"Fourth," Winston chirped. "I'm a natural. Even as a little kid I always spotted shooting stars. I wanted to be an astronaut."

Elizabeth leaned back on her elbows. "It's not too late. SVU has a great astrophysics department. Why not go for it?"

Winston grinned and looked down at his high-top sneakers. "I'm afraid of heights."

Elizabeth laughed. "*That* would be a problem." She paused thoughtfully. "I think being an astronaut would be too lonely for me. Too much open, empty space, and your loved ones so far away."

Winston nodded. "That would get to me too."

Elizabeth turned to study her friend. "Where's Wendy tonight? Since you've been staying with her for the summer, I'm not used to seeing one of you without the other."

Winston drew in a long breath of air. "She's got an appointment with a lawyer."

Elizabeth stared at Winston. "What for?"

Winston flinched and ran a hand through his curly hair. "Divorce."

"No!" Elizabeth cried, sitting bolt upright on the stairs. "I thought she and Pedro were the perfect couple. They're crazy about each other."

Winston shook his head and toyed with the turned-up edge of his khakis, dislodging a cuff-load of sand. "I know," he said with a groan. "They *are* perfect. That's what I keep telling Wendy. But she's feeling neglected. Pedro's tour keeps getting extended. Wendy doesn't know when she's going to see him again, and now she's not sure if she even loves him anymore."

"But divorce?" Elizabeth echoed. The word hung in the air like a bad smell. "That's so final. Can't they go for marriage counseling or something first?"

Winston shrugged. "Tonight's appointment is for informal advice only, from one of her family's friends. I'm hoping the woman will talk some sense into her."

Elizabeth nodded sadly and hugged her

jeans-clad knees. *What is going on?* she wondered. Last summer Wendy and Pedro, and Jessica and Ben, had all been madly in love. *And Ryan and I, well, we had a very deep, intense understanding,* she thought with a bittersweet smile. But this summer it seemed as if Sweet Valley Shore was a jinx on everybody.

"What's going on with you, Liz?" Winston asked, interrupting her thoughts. "You seem a little down yourself."

Elizabeth sighed. Now it was her turn to play with her sneakers. "Ryan is acting really weird and cold." She brushed a strand of her golden blond hair from her face, tucking it back under her hood. "I missed an important dinner date with him last night, but when I tried to apologize, he wouldn't even listen."

Winston patted her arm. "Don't worry too much. You know Ryan. He's always been moody. He's probably going through one of his Ryan things."

Elizabeth sniffed back a tear. "I don't know. I thought we'd gotten beyond that. It doesn't make sense for him to be cold. I don't understand it."

Winston laughed. "Maybe he thought you were cooling on him. So he's reeling you back in with what attracted you in the first place—the mysterious, brooding guy."

Elizabeth rolled her sea green eyes. "Winston, that's not true at all. I was attracted to Ryan because he was . . ." *Mysterious and brooding*, she realized.

Winston nodded, as if reading her mind. "You girls always go for the silent, serious types, leaving clowns like me with the job of being the perpetual shoulder to cry on." He patted the shoulder of his Windbreaker. "Go on. Have a good cry."

Elizabeth laughed and gave him a soft push. "If my memory serves me, you've had more than your share of amazing girlfriends."

He shoved her back playfully. "And you've had some amazing boyfriends. I'm sure Ryan will get over whatever he's dealing with and realize how lucky he is."

Elizabeth crossed her fingers. "I hope you're right. But the way he acted today—" She hesitated as the sound of the main lifeguard tower door slamming echoed in her mind. "It's almost as if he . . . *hates* me." Her voice broke. She looked at Winston, tears gathering in her eyes.

"C'mon," he said, motioning her toward him and rolling his eyes playfully. A small, sympathetic smile wobbled on his lips.

"Thanks." She sniffled, relenting and leaning her head on his shoulder for a good long cry.

*   *   *

Ryan shifted uneasily as he stood on Sunnyside Boulevard, one of the seedier sections of Sweet Valley Shore. He nonchalantly tossed a quarter into the air. "Tails, the meeting," he murmured. "Heads, the bottle." But as the coin came down, he ignored the outcome and threw it back into space.

Across the street from him stood the two opposing forces. The white stucco Methodist church on the left and the liquor store, with its glaring neon sign, on the right. He studied the two facades as they both pulled at him with equal force.

Laughter made him step back into the shadows under the broken streetlamp. He flipped up the collar of his black leather jacket to obscure his face. A group of people he knew streamed past to cross the road to the church. They were heading for the 10 P.M. meeting of Alcoholics Anonymous.

Two days ago he would have been joining them. Ryan tossed the coin again into the air. "Tails, the meeting. Heads, the bottle." Again he didn't look at the outcome.

Two days ago was a long time. He studied the garish facade of the liquor store. Multicolored bottles of booze lined one window. *Eenie meenie minie moe,* he thought, *whiskey, rum, or gin to go.*

He clutched the quarter tightly in his palm.

There was one more choice he could make, he realized. He could call Elizabeth. She could pick him up after the meeting and help him get through that first, torturous night of sobriety.

Ryan snorted with derision, remembering her empty promise about meeting him at his celebration dinner. "Elizabeth," he spat. "Fat chance of her help. That's like throwing a lifesaver to a drowning man—the cherry-flavored variety."

Ryan waited until the traffic slowed on the boulevard and dashed across. He stood rooted to the pavement, equidistant from the church and the liquor store. It was a little after ten, and he knew the meeting would be under way. If he were to enter the room, he would have to raise his hand and claim he was one day back. The faces turning to him would be sad, but full of compassion. There was no shame in slipping as long as you tried again.

Ryan threw the coin up into the air for the last time. It spiraled and glinted in the passing headlight of a car, landing with a soft whack in his palm. He turned it over on the back of his other hand. "Heads." He sighed and walked the few short steps to his right, pushing open the door to the liquor store.

Maybe he would get sober tomorrow.

Chapter
Five

"Focus," Jessica reminded herself, rubbing the sleep from her eyes. "Gotta stay sharp." She took a sip of hot black coffee from her plastic foam cup and leaned back in one of the white, wooden lifeguard chairs at Tower 3. It was an especially bright Tuesday morning; Miranda was off getting a bottle of water from the main lifeguard tower, so for the moment Jessica was alone at her post.

The beach was already crowded with people, their beach blankets and towels stretching up and down the shore like an enormous patchwork quilt. The morning waves were unusually calm, barely cresting before gently gliding to shore.

But mild days like this can be deceptive, she remembered. During training Ryan had told them time and again about what could happen when a lifeguard let down his or her guard, even for a minute. And calm days always made it easy to let down your guard.

"Hey!" Jessica said anxiously, her attention drawn to a bright yellow speedboat that had appeared on the water almost out of nowhere. The skipper was obviously joyriding, maneuvering the boat in wide arcs so it would cut back on its own wake, causing the boat to bounce violently on the water. "That hunk of metal's way too close to the bathing areas," she realized with alarm.

Jessica sat forward, her heart thumping against her chest, and grabbed her binoculars, training them on the speedboat. Three young men were laughing and gesturing as they clowned around at the steering wheel.

"Jerks," Jessica muttered. Suddenly the boat swerved wildly. "Oh no!" The boat was heading directly for the shore, running at full throttle. Jessica glanced quickly through her binoculars again. It was obvious that not one of the jokers playing seaman was paying any attention to where they were going.

Jessica scrambled to her feet on top of the large lifeguard chair, frantically blowing her whistle and crossing her arms above her head to get their attention. The speedboat was barely thirty feet away from the outermost group of swimmers. Among them was a little girl floating on an inner tube.

Jessica felt her guts twist in her stomach. *If that boat doesn't veer off,* her mind raced, *it's going to hit that little girl!*

The sound of her whistle had alerted the two neighboring lifeguard stands that there was trouble on the water. Out of the corner of her eye Jessica could see the flash of red streaking down the beach—Theo Moore. But it was no use. Theo's position on the horizon was too low to catch the attention of the guys on the speedboat. *This is it, Jess,* she thought. *I'm the only thing standing between that boat and a total disaster!*

Almost on pure instinct she turned and grabbed her beach towel. The bright red towel was the biggest warning signal at her station. She began waving it wildly, praying the rectangle of color would catch one of the boaters' eyes.

"C'mon," Jessica whispered desperately, whipping the towel back and forth. In the water some of the swimmers had noticed the boat and were frantically attempting to swim toward shore. But none of them had thought to pull the little girl on the inner tube to safety. She was still floating on the water, practically a sitting duck. *Look up,* Jessica pleaded mentally.

With the boat no more than ten feet from the little girl, one of the guys finally glanced up, his eye caught by the big red towel. He flashed a goofy grin as Jessica frantically pointed at the little girl before him. The guy looked down. Even at a distance Jessica could see the color drain from his face as he spotted the floating inner tube. He lurched forward and yanked the wheel, spinning the speedboat in a tight arc, missing the little girl by inches.

"It worked!" Jessica screamed, relief flooding her. But before Jessica's horrified eyes, the boat's wake came crashing over the inner tube, capsizing the little girl. She disappeared beneath the now turbulent water. The empty inner tube was left bobbing ominously on the water.

Jessica grabbed the red rescue buoy hanging on the arm of her chair and leaped off the lifeguard stand, her legs moving almost before she hit the sand. She tore to the shore and dove into the water, her limbs expertly jackknifing through the waves.

She came up about twelve feet offshore, not missing a stroke as she honed in on the inner tube floating up ahead. She cut through the water at full force, using her arms and legs to propel her forward. *Breathe, two, three,* the metronome in her head told her. She was only a few feet from the inner tube now.

Jessica held the end of the rescue buoy's coiled rope and took a quick breath before diving into the murky ocean depths. The salt water stung at her eyes. Beneath the waves there was no sound, only the roaring pressure of the sea and her own heart pounding in her chest. She looked around frantically, pushing herself deeper into the cold water. *Nothing.* No sign of the girl. And now her air was running out.

With two powerful kicks she broke the surface of the water, ready for another gulp of precious oxygen before returning to her search. But as she came up, she saw a head of black hair and a telltale red bathing suit shoot up from the water about halfway to the shore. Priya Rahman had the little girl clutched firmly in her arms.

Jessica tried to relax her knotted stomach. She knew that saving lives was the bottom line, but she couldn't help but feel irritated that Priya had yet again stolen her thunder. But if not for Jessica's quick thinking and attention-getting actions from Tower 3, the girl might not have been saved at all. *A classic teamwork save,* she thought begrudgingly. *At least Priya didn't trip me before I could make it to the water this time.*

As her exhausted legs found the ocean floor, she saw Ben rushing to aid Priya as she carried the unconscious girl up onto the shore. Jessica quickly pulled in her rescue buoy, coiling the rope around it.

"Daria! Daria!" the little girl's mother cried as Ben and Priya began working on the child. Jessica jogged up to the crowd that had gathered, just in time to hear the little girl splutter and cough—she was out of danger! "Daria!" the young mother exclaimed, her voice now flooded with relief.

Jessica pushed through the cheering crowd, beaming. "Great teamwork," she enthused, stopping before her fellow lifeguards.

There was a snort of derision. "Yeah, great teamwork," Priya sneered. "If Ben and I hadn't come along, you'd still be playing duck-duck-goose in the water."

"Yeah, Jessica," Ben chimed in. "Blowing your whistle to signal for other lifeguards to do your dirty work isn't what we consider team-work. Priya and I were the team on this save."

Jessica stepped back as if she'd been slapped. "Are you serious?" she cried. Hadn't they seen what happened with the motorboat? "If it wasn't for me, that little girl would be *mincemeat* right now!"

The little girl, now safely in her mother's arms, looked up at Jessica with wide brown eyes—then she burst into tears. The girl's mother glared at Jessica indignantly.

"Jessica," Ben hissed, scowling at her. "She's shook up enough as it is. She doesn't need you frightening her."

The crowd started to murmur angrily.

"Who's this washout?"

"Stop causing trouble, miss."

"Honestly, scaring a poor little girl like that."

"No class. What a shame."

"Really, Jessica," Priya snapped. "Get back to your post. Ben and I have this situation under control."

Jessica's mouth dropped open as she was shoved aside by the crowd. *I'm nobody to them,* she thought. *Just another blonde in a red swimsuit.* She turned and stomped angrily back to Tower 3. "How can this be?" she glowered. "I *did* help save that little girl. What am I, invisible?"

The young woman woke in her tiny, furnished room at the VistaView Apartments, knowing it would be an important day. "Stuart knows too," she whispered. Together she and Stuart were moving toward something. An understanding. An agreement. Without words, without contact. A love like theirs didn't need such mundane forms of communication. *After yesterday, after the fire-walking episode, it's obvious,* she thought. *Our hearts spoke. He knows I'm back.*

"And I would be with him now if it weren't for *her,*" she snarled. The young woman threw off the tattered bedspread covering her legs and sat up on the single bed. "It's all *Nina's* fault." She twisted the hem of her long cotton nightgown. "I should be at Stuart's, waking up in his arms right now."

89

She closed her eyes and imagined herself wrapped in silken sheets, luxuriating on a queen-size water bed as bright sunshine streamed through an open window. She could see Stuart waking her with one of the passionate kisses that only he could give. "Stuart," she murmured, opening her eyes.

The fresh shock of reality made her bite down hard on her lip. "Nina deserves this place, not me," she spat, looking around the darkened, furnished room with loathing. A hint of natural light fought its way through a small, grime-caked window. She reached forward and flipped the wall switch beside the creaky single bed. The harsh glare of a bare bulb illuminated the gloomy furnishings.

"Maybe after I move in with Stuart, Nina can live here," the young woman proposed gleefully.

She stood and moved to the one other piece of furniture in the room—a scarred, messy desk that supported the cracked remains of a mirror. She grimaced at her fractured reflection in the shattered glass. A full inch of dark roots stood out against her short, platinum blond hair.

"Not again," she said with a groan. She'd wanted to get an early start this morning, not waste time bleaching her hair. Like her memories of the past, the dark brown kept sprouting up—a horrid reminder of all the terrible things that had befallen her. Before.

"Forget the past," she shouted, clutching her temples as a stabbing pain shot through her head. The voices from the past didn't want to leave her in peace. She gritted her teeth. "Nothing that happened before I met Stuart matters."

She took a deep breath and held it, clutching either side of the desk, willing herself to remain calm. "Must stay in control," she cautioned herself. She couldn't afford any more trouble with the landlady or she'd find herself thrown out onto the street. Smashing the mirror had been nearly the last straw.

The young woman guided her eyes to the newspaper picture she'd tacked next to the mirror. She gazed lovingly at the grainy photograph of Stuart leaning against a colorful Boogie board. The headline read, Surfer-Turned-Success-Story.

"Stuart, my love," she whispered. "Why are you so blind? Don't you remember how beautiful we were together? How right?"

She wrapped her arms around her body, recreating the feel of Stuart's strong arms as he'd twirled her across the dance floor on the night they met. "Pure bliss," she moaned softly as she swayed to the imaginary music.

But then the image of Nina popped into her mind and the sweet memories disintegrated. "You've ruined everything, Nina," she growled. "But I won't let you get away with it. Not today!"

The young woman grabbed the bottle of peroxide

from the bottom drawer and sprinted down the hallway. "It's an emergency," she screamed, banging on the door of the communal bathroom. She pushed an elderly man aside as he emerged from the room. "Out of my way!"

She poured the bleach directly onto her head, not bothering with protective gloves. The painful burning and sharp, putrid smell helped her to focus her mind. *Stuart.* In twenty minutes she'd be ready. She walked back down to her room and sat cross-legged on the bed.

Twenty minutes was a long time when you wanted to be somewhere else. But she was used to waiting. She was as patient as a spider.

Suddenly a brilliant thought came to her. Now that Stuart was aware of her, she could break the silence. She would send him a letter—a love letter.

The young woman smiled, licking her lips in anticipation. "Stuart knows I'm here for him. Deep down he wants someone to help push Nina away."

Her light brown eyes sparkled as she imagined Nina crying, desperately trying to clutch at Stuart as he shook her off. Fully energized, the young woman reached under her bed for her journal and a pen. Her hand trembled in excitement as she poised her pen over the paper. She shook her head to steady herself, sending spots of peroxide across the room. Taking a deep breath, she began.

> Dearest Stuart,
> I haven't forgotten you or the beautiful times we shared and I know it's not your fault that we're not together now because you've been TEMPTED and TRICKED!!! I should never have strayed from your side even for a second and I was a fool to let someone else blind you to our TRUE LOVE!!! I dreamed of you last night—imagined waking beside you again—our bodies pressed close NO ONE else will ever mean as much to me as YOU do or as much to YOU as I after seeing you yesterday. I KNOW you understand that we will be together soon my love, don't despair and then we will NEVER EVER be apart again.

She sat back and studied the note. It was short, but sweet. Just enough to let Stuart know she'd be with him soon. She leaned down from the bed and picked up last night's discarded clothing. Smiling, she pulled her favorite ruby red lipstick from the pocket of her jeans. She thickly coated her lips before signing the bottom of the letter with a lipstick kiss.

"Perfect," she pronounced, and then headed for the bathroom. As she turned on the faucets and adjusted the old plumbing to run warm, it crossed her mind that she could almost leave it at that. The letter would open Stuart's eyes and make him see how he'd been tricked. The letter would free him from Nina. But then her eyes narrowed. *Why take chances?* she thought. *The way to help Stuart is to make sure Nina Harper is out of his hair forever.*

She leaned forward over the sink. "I'm going to wash that girl right out of my hair," she cackled as she rinsed out the bleach. "Wash her right out of this *life!*"

"Hey, Liz," Miranda called up from the base of Elizabeth's lifeguard chair. "Ryan's called a lunchtime meeting at the main tower."

Elizabeth stood up, knocking the delicious-looking Brie and tomato sandwich she'd made that morning off the wooden chair and into the sand. "Oh no," she groaned. "And I was starving too."

Miranda stood at the foot of the chair and stared at the sandwich. "And it looks like a total loss, folks," she announced in an excited sportscaster's voice. "Elizabeth's sandwich is down. Down for the count. This is one sandwich that won't be getting up."

Elizabeth laughed and scampered down the tower to join Miranda. "Yuck," she complained, picking up her sandwich and regretfully dropping it in the nearest trash can. She wiped her slender hands on her regulation white nylon jacket and walked back to Miranda. "Did Ryan say what the meeting's about?"

Miranda shook her head. "Nope. Just that it's happening ASAP."

Elizabeth frowned as she unwedged her laceless cross trainers from between two of the chair's wooden slats and quickly slid them on. *What can the big hurry be?* she wondered, feeling a shiver of trepidation. After Ryan's cold behavior yesterday, she didn't know what to expect. "ASAP it is," she grumbled as she and Miranda began jogging down the beach.

As they approached the main tower, Elizabeth could see that most of the Sweet Valley Shore lifeguards were already gathered around the deck. She and Miranda joined Nina, who was leaning against the wooden railing and eating an apple. Next to her Ben was joking with his buddy Theo, one of this summer's rookies.

"Hi, Nina." Elizabeth stared hungrily as Nina took another bite of her apple. "Mmm . . . that sure looks delicious."

Nina looked up and smiled. "Have a bite, but don't take too much. It's all I have. I accidentally dumped the rest of my lunch into the sand."

Elizabeth and Miranda exchanged looks and laughed. "You too?" Elizabeth asked. "I hope this meeting is important because it's ruined two good meals."

Nina raised her eyebrows. "It must be. I've never known Ryan to call an impromptu meeting like this. He'd better be quick, though. Jessica and Priya are the only two lifeguards manning the fort."

"You're kidding!" Elizabeth swallowed her bite of apple and flinched. "That sounds like a recipe for disaster. What if they meet up in the water?"

"They already have," Nina replied, taking back her apple. "After this morning's rescue controversy, I'm betting Jessica will give the first dunk."

Ben leaned in. "No way," he sneered. "Jessica might try, but Priya can swim circles around her."

Elizabeth snorted. She wasn't going to get caught up in Jessica and Ben's little competition. *Keep it light,* she told herself. "You don't know my sister," she said teasingly. "Hell hath no fury—"

"Like a woman scorned," Ben cut in. "Yes, the archetypal scorned woman and the paternalistic reliance of the traditional academy on that oversimplified notion of female identity is central to Priya's dissertation."

Elizabeth rolled her blue-green eyes as Miranda leaned forward and made a gagging gesture. "Is there anything Priya can't do, Ben?" Miranda asked sarcastically.

Ben smiled and tipped back his baseball cap thoughtfully. "Not that I know of."

How about showing a little humility? Elizabeth thought, feeling her own gag reflex acting up.

"Attention, please," Ryan demanded, cutting through the group's chattering. "I have an announcement to make."

Elizabeth gave a start as she took in Ryan's appearance. He looked disheveled and ill at ease as he leaned against the wooden railing. His light brown hair was a tangled mess, and his usually smooth face was covered with stubble. She couldn't make out his expression behind his dark glasses, but his creased forehead told her it wasn't good.

"What is it, Ryan?" she gasped. "Has someone died?"

Ryan's lips curled into an unpleasant sneer. "No, Elizabeth," he replied in a strange, flat voice. "Just the opposite." He turned away from her and addressed the rest of the lifeguards. "I've been giving this a lot of thought," he began, "and the bottom line is, my heart's not in the job anymore. It's too stressful, and

I've realized I really need to relax for a while."

Elizabeth felt the air go out of her lungs. *Not into the job?* she thought in amazement. *What is he talking about?* "Ryan," she cried, "you've never discussed this with me."

Ryan turned to her, his body shaking with barely concealed anger. "No, Elizabeth, I haven't. And I would appreciate not being interrupted again. If you can't control your outbursts while I conduct this meeting, then please go back to your post."

Elizabeth started to protest, but the words caught in her throat as Ryan turned away from her with a dismissive wave of his hand. "As of this moment," he announced, "I'm stepping down as head lifeguard and transferring all my duties to Nina."

"Me? The head lifeguard?" Elizabeth heard Nina gasp. Elizabeth couldn't believe her ears either. "You must be kidding," Nina continued. "I can't take on that responsibility."

Ryan's scowling face was suddenly transformed into a supportive smile. "Of course you can, Nina. You're the best lifeguard we have."

"But Ryan," Ben called out, "will you continue to man a post?"

"Probably not," Ryan told them. He leaned back on the railing, nonchalantly crossing his arms. "Nina has the ultimate authority and responsibility for our crew. For the time being," he added, "I'm taking the day off. And the next. And the next."

Elizabeth was reeling as if she'd been struck. Was this some kind of joke? Being head lifeguard was more important to Ryan than anything. And he was acting as if he didn't have a care in the world. *How can he be so calm after dropping that bomb on us?* she thought in astonishment. *This certainly isn't the Ryan Taylor I love.*

"I'm glad that's over," Ryan muttered as he walked back toward his room in the main lifeguard tower. He would start packing up his stuff and move out by the end of the week. He'd seen a boardinghouse down on Vine Street with a room he could afford. And if that cut into his drink money too much, there was always a park bench or a place to sleep in the dunes. He wasn't proud.

A soft tap on the door made him turn around. He felt his heart sink as he recognized the slender curves on the other side of the screen.

I knew I should have locked that door, he thought. "What do you want?" he called out.

Elizabeth came into the room, her brow knitted with concern. "Ryan," she whispered, reaching out to him. "What's going on?"

Ryan stepped back to avoid her hands. "Elizabeth," he said with exasperation, "I just explained that. Don't you listen?"

She shook her head, tears glittering on her long eyelashes. "I heard you. I just don't understand."

Ryan gritted his teeth in frustration. He was angry that she was questioning him, but even more angry that the sight of her still made his temperature rise and his heart flip. "Let me spell it out for you," he said coldly, pushing any remaining feelings of tenderness aside. "I can't take the responsibility anymore, OK? I don't care. Do you want me to stay on as head lifeguard with that attitude? Don't you think that's stupid and dangerous?"

Elizabeth stared at him, her eyes wide with anguish. "But *why* don't you care, Ryan? What's happened? This can't all be because I missed our date the other night."

He shook his head, his thoughts swirling. His mouth felt parched, and more than anything he wanted a drink. "Do you have to analyze everything to death?"

"But if we talk," she faltered, her voice pleading, "maybe I can help."

Ryan felt his throat catch. Part of him wanted to reach out to her—to let her help him the way he knew she wanted to. But that would mean being back in the straitjacket of responsibility. No liquor. No fun.

"Forget it," he growled, glaring at her. "I don't have to explain myself to you. And if you're so concerned about the lifeguard staffing, I suggest you get back to your post and start doing your job."

Elizabeth let out the strangled cry of a small, hurt animal. She turned away and stumbled toward the door.

"That's right," he shouted after her, despite the twisting pain in his heart. "Go! Let me get on with my life!"

Chapter Six

"Wendy, why are you sitting in the dark?" Winston asked, jogging down the three steps into the Palomas' spacious sunken living room in his brand-new purple tracksuit. He pulled open the blinds that covered the huge French windows, allowing the bright sun to stream in from the expansive, colorful garden.

"It's a beautiful day! I just jogged twenty—well, maybe two miles. You'd think it was the middle of the night in here, not early afternoon." He gave a self-satisfied grunt at the now brightly lit room and turned to look at Wendy, who sat curled up in the corner of the white leather couch.

She whimpered and buried her face in her hands.

"What is it?" Winston asked, running over

and dropping down to his knees in front of her. "Did something happen?"

Wendy shook her head and burrowed deeper into the couch. She was still in the blue-and-white-striped sundress he'd seen her wearing yesterday. Winston realized with a start that he'd gone to sleep before Wendy came home last night. From the crumpled look of her clothes and tired eyes, she might not have gone to bed at all.

"Wendy, have you been in here all night?" Winston had gotten up early to check on a few job leads and then gone for a long run. He hadn't seen Wendy for breakfast that morning, so he'd assumed she'd either gotten up and out of the house early or was still sleeping. But now he realized she must have been crying her eyes out the whole time. "Wendy, talk to me!"

Wendy sniffled once and dabbed at her eyes with a crumpled tissue. "There's nothing to talk about. My marriage is over."

Winston stood up and took the seat next to her, wrapping his arm around her trembling shoulders. "That's not true," he protested, hugging her. "Come on, what's gotten you so upset?"

Wendy's voice faltered slightly. "She said I have grounds for divorce based on irreconcilable differences."

"Who said that? What are you talking about?"

103

Wendy grabbed a pillow, hugging it close to her. "The lawyer I talked to last night. She said I wouldn't have any trouble getting a decree against Pedro."

"What?" Winston gasped. He'd forgotten all about the lawyer. But that woman was supposed to be a friend of Wendy's family. Winston had assumed she'd try to convince Wendy she was making a mistake, not give her a legal argument for divorce! "That's crazy. What does she know about marriage anyway? She's a divorce lawyer. Of *course* she wants you to get divorced—that's how she gets paid!"

Wendy shook her head and pointed to a stack of glossy women's magazines that covered the bamboo coffee table. "They all say it too."

Winston leaped to his feet. "What do they say? Wendy and Pedro Paloma should divorce? What are they, gossip rags?"

Wendy gave him a weak smile. "We're not that famous a couple. Most people don't even know I exist." She reached over and picked up a magazine off the top of the stack. Sighing, she thumbed through it until she reached the page she wanted and held it up for Winston to see. "It's a test."

Winston bent down, squinting. He didn't wear his glasses when he jogged, and unless something was really close, everything looked like squiggly lines to him. "You'll have to read it to me. I can't see."

Wendy pulled the magazine toward her. "It says, 'Are you headed for divorce?'"

Winston made a face. "How would they know?"

Wendy sighed. "They asked a bunch of questions, and I answered them." Her bottom lip began to quiver as she started to read. "'Do you share common interests and goals?'" She looked up at Winston. "No. Pedro has his music. I have nothing." She looked back down at the magazine. "'Do you share at least one romantic meal together a week?'" Wendy grimaced. "I'm lucky if we grab a pizza together once a month." She scanned the page again. "'Do you feel that your partner appreciates you?' Maybe if I ever saw him, but since I don't, I have to answer no."

Winston grabbed the magazine away from her and tossed it aside. "That's one magazine. The person who wrote that probably doesn't know the first thing—"

"No!" Wendy cried. "I took *ten* tests. Ten different magazines. Look." She began sifting through the magazines on the pile. "*Psychology for Her. Virtual Woman. The Female Perspective.* Each time Pedro and I failed. We're in the lowest percentile in every category. It's a wonder we're married at all."

Winston started to pace around the room, following the geometric lines of the large Afghan carpet covering the tiled floor. *Ten tests,* he thought, *ten different magazines and a lawyer. No wonder Wendy is feeling doubt.* But Winston had seen the way Wendy looked at Pedro and the way Pedro looked at her. *That's something the lawyer and the magazines don't know about. It has to be worth something.*

"Wendy, who buys those magazines?" he asked quickly.

Wendy looked up from where she was sitting, her eyelids red rimmed from tears. "Everybody. All kinds of women. Housewives. Businesswomen. Students."

"OK, but wouldn't you say that the type of marriage they have in mind when they invent those tests is pretty conventional? Wouldn't you say that they were catering to the majority of their readers?"

Wendy shrugged and toyed with the tassel on the pillow. "I guess so."

"So wouldn't you say, then, that those magazine tests don't really apply to you and Pedro?" Winston turned on the heel of his sneaker, took two long steps until he stood before her, and banged his fist on the coffee table in his best courtroom-lawyer imitation. "I mean, you and Pedro aren't exactly an average couple! He's an artist. Have they made allowances for that in these tests? Do they ask how many spouses have had songs written for them? I bet not! I bet if they invented a test for the type of people you and Pedro are, you'd be in the top percentile. I rest my case."

Wendy smiled sadly. "Thanks for trying, Perry Mason. But I think these magazines and that lawyer I saw last night know a lot more about which marriages stand a chance than you or I."

Winston shook his head. "OK. If you won't take my word for it, can we at least seek some other opinions?" There was no way Winston was going to give up on his friend's marriage without a fight.

Wendy sighed. "If you insist, but my mind is pretty much made up. This marriage is a loser."

"Why me?" Nina fumed as she angrily scanned the faces of the remaining lifeguards gathered around her. She'd had her whole summer mapped out. Sun, sleep, and exercise had been her main signposts. And despite her earlier vow of a manless summer, meeting sexy Stu Kirkwood had turned out to be the cherry on top of the sundae. *If I take on the extra responsibility of being head lifeguard,* she fretted, *then when will I find time for any of those things? Especially Stu!*

She glared at the entrance of the main tower's living quarters, where Ryan had disappeared a few minutes before. "I have half a mind to go in there and have it out with him," she muttered. *And I would have,* she thought, *if Elizabeth hadn't rushed in there first.* Those two obviously had a lot to talk about, judging from the way Ryan had curtly dismissed Elizabeth during his resignation speech.

"Come on, Nina," Theo called, jumping down from the railing and heading for the wooden stairs. "You'll be great."

"Yeah," Ben added, knocking back his baseball cap at a jaunty angle. "I wouldn't worry about it."

Nina turned on them, her eyes flashing. "That's easy for you two to say. You haven't been sentenced to more work for the entire summer."

Miranda laughed and patted Nina's back. "We're really proud of you, boss. We're sure you'll do a wonderful job."

Nina crossed her arms angrily over her red lifeguard suit, blocking everyone's way to the wooden stairs. "Of course I'll do a wonderful job," she snapped. "It's not about being great! It's about not wanting all my time taken up."

Ben grinned, ducking around her and running down the steps. "See you later, chief."

Nina glowered at his strong, tanned back as

he loped off across the sand, whistling a happy tune. She watched, feeling her cocoa brown skin practically turn green with envy as he climbed back up to his post with Priya. *He doesn't have to worry about his free time,* she thought angrily. *His summer isn't now officially ruined.*

Miranda smiled sweetly and tried to wiggle her way around Nina's other side.

"Where do you think you're going?" Nina demanded.

Miranda grinned. "To tell Jessica your good news?" She faked a left and scooted past Nina on the right before Nina had a chance to stop her.

"I'll give you good news," Nina yelled, chasing her down the last two steps. "I'll make sure the two of you end up on beach patrol all night long!"

Miranda tossed her silky brown hair back as she laughed. "We won't mind. At least it will keep us away from Priya!"

Theo cleared his throat.

Nina whipped around. He was the last one left on the deck and didn't show signs of trying to escape. "What do you want?"

"Um," he started, toying with the lifeguard whistle that dangled just above his washboard abs. "Ryan and I had an understanding."

Nina narrowed her eyes. "What are you talking about?"

Theo gingerly walked down the steps until he was level with Nina on the wooden walkway. "I told Ryan at the beginning of the week that I wouldn't be able to be here tomorrow."

Nina put her hands on her hips. "So? Why are you telling me?"

Theo deftly stepped around her, giving himself a clear passage to the beach. He looked back at her with an impish grin. "Because now that you're the head lifeguard instead of Ryan"—he blurted as his muscular legs took off running—"you'll have to fill in for me."

"You must be crazy!" Nina screamed, chasing him a few yards down the beach. "I'll put you on double shifts for this."

Theo's laughter stung her ears as he jogged away to safety.

"Arggh!" Nina shrieked. "I'm going to kill you, Ryan Taylor!" She was *this* close to doing it too. But with the way she felt at that moment, she couldn't even bear to look at Ryan, let alone tear him limb from limb. Exasperated, she started trudging back to her post.

"Four more hours of duty," she muttered, looking at her waterproof watch. "There's *got* to be some way I can get Ryan to change his mind. If I don't, my summer's ruined!"

*   *   *

"Nina, wait!" Elizabeth yelled, spying her best friend's bright red lifeguard suit moving through the sea of colorful bikinis and one-pieces near the water's edge.

Nina stopped and turned, shielding her eyes from the midday glare.

"I'm glad I caught up with you," Elizabeth exclaimed as she reached her. If she couldn't get Ryan to explain his sudden strange behavior, maybe Nina could enlighten her. Nina had known him a lot longer than Elizabeth had. "This whole thing has got me worried sick. What's going on with Ryan?"

"Who?" Nina asked distractedly, starting to walk again.

Who? Elizabeth echoed silently. *How could Nina ask that? Who just turned both our summers upside down?* "Ryan!" she cried. "I can't understand his behavior at all. It's as if he can't stand us being in the same room together. And why would he give up being head lifeguard? It's his whole life."

Nina shook her head and stepped nimbly away as a wave pushed up onto the shore. "Who knows. But this promotion is *not* what I had in mind. He'll be off having fun while I'm working double time. I don't think it's fair at all."

Elizabeth tightened her ponytail. "I tried talking to him, but he's acting as if it isn't any of my business."

"Hey, no running!" Nina suddenly shouted. She grabbed her whistle and gave two quick warning blasts—a code that indicated to the other lifeguards it wasn't an emergency.

Elizabeth looked up to see two young boys halt in their tracks. Three empty beach chairs lay toppled in their wake. The older of the two pointed at her. "She was running a second ago," he explained.

Nina growled. "That was official lifeguard business. Now walk."

The two boys made faces but left without causing trouble.

Nina rolled her eyes. "I really don't want this job."

Elizabeth sighed. "I can't understand why Ryan didn't tell me he was going to quit. You would think I would have known what he was planning. But no." She adjusted a shoulder strap on her lifeguard suit. "I was as much in the dark as the rest of you."

Nina bent down and picked up an empty soda can. "Being head lifeguard will leave me no time for—" She stopped suddenly. "For exercising and regaining my peace of mind after what Bryan did to me. But I guess that's out." She took a few quick strides up the beach to toss the can in a metal garbage bin, Elizabeth following close behind.

Elizabeth shrugged. As much as she felt for Nina, she couldn't let herself get too worked up about her troubles—not with Ryan turning into a total stranger right before her eyes. "Ryan is acting as if we're nothing to each other. Yesterday morning he slammed the door in my face when I tried to talk to him. I know something's going on. I just don't know what."

Nina kicked at a piece of driftwood distractedly. "Then there's all the paperwork I'll have to do after my shift every evening. I'll be lucky if I'm done before midnight. And as if that's not bad enough, Theo's planning to be off tomorrow. We'll be totally shorthanded."

Suddenly Elizabeth felt anger flare up and overtake her. Nina wasn't even listening to her. *Nina's only worried about herself,* she thought. *How can she be so selfish?*

Elizabeth stopped and squarely faced her friend. "Have you heard a word I've said, Nina? You're going on and on about how this is going to affect *you,* but what about Ryan? Who knows what's going on with him. Don't you even care?"

Nina turned to her, her dark eyes blazing. "Me! Have *you* heard anything *you've* said? It's all about poor Liz. 'Ryan isn't paying attention to *me.* Ryan isn't telling *me* what's going on.' You don't really care about what's happening

113

with Ryan either. You're just worried whether he's still your *boyfriend* or not. So don't get on my case about not caring. You're supposed to be in love with him, but all you're talking about is how it affects *you!*"

Elizabeth stepped back, stung and speechless. *How dare you say that!* her mind raged. But before she could say a word in her defense, Nina had turned on her heels and was running down the beach.

Ryan whistled a soundless tune as he relaxed on the deck of the main tower. The slow slap of the waves against the jetty was mesmerizing. "A nice nap might be in order," he murmured.

He glanced up when he heard the shrieks of an insistent gull. *You and me, pal,* he thought. *We've got the life.* He leaned back, crossing his arms behind his head. No more responsibility. Plenty of free time. *I should have passed off this job weeks ago.*

Suddenly out of the corner of his eye he caught a blurred reflection. Ryan sat up with a bang. Two hands were flailing just beyond where the waves broke. The image was blurred through his exhaustion and hangover, but he was sure someone was struggling.

He leaped off the wooden platform and started running toward the water. It wasn't until he was halfway there that he realized he'd not only neglected to signal the other lifeguards that he was going in for a save but he hadn't brought along his flotation device either.

Go back! the rational part of his brain told him. *Follow procedure. Take proper precautions.* But the bravado part of his brain wouldn't listen. *Make the save, Ryan. You're a pro.*

Gritting his teeth, he dove into the sea and scraped his arms on the bottom. The pain sent a shock to his sluggish brain. He'd misjudged the water's depth.

He coughed and spluttered as he fought to regain his balance. *How did that happen?* his mind cried out. He'd done that same dive a million times. Had the tides suddenly changed?

Shaking his head to clear it, Ryan took a deep gulp of air. But before he could plunge back into the surf, a huge breaker crashed over his head, slamming him back onto the shallow bottom. The pressure of the churning water roared in his ears.

Ryan propelled himself up, realizing with a start that he was now facing the shore. He whipped around to see another huge swell suspended above him. He gasped, ducking his head under the breaking wave and avoiding the brunt of its power by a split second.

He plowed his way underwater as the whitecap

crashed harmlessly behind him. Shaken and confused, he emerged in the calm water beyond the break lines. Ryan looked around, momentarily dazed, desperately trying to reorient himself by treading water until he had a fix on the person he'd seen from the shore.

He quickly saw that the two flailing hands had now turned into four. *Hold on, folks. I'm coming,* he thought. Ryan stroked powerfully in their direction, realizing vaguely that the two potential victims were close to the sandbar. Maybe they'd slipped off into the stronger outlying current.

"Hey," he heard one of the swimmers say, laughing. *Laughter,* Ryan thought. *That's a bad sign. People often get hysterical when they're drowning.* Ryan swam harder, reaching what turned out to be a couple thrashing in the water, their arms locked together.

"Don't panic," Ryan cried, diving under the surface and attempting to wrench the pair apart. The woman was obviously terrified and trying to climb on top of the man. Nothing could be more dangerous! Ryan dunked her to subdue her, locking his strong arm around her neck.

"Hey, get your hands off my girlfriend, you creep!" shouted her companion. Ryan felt a sharp blow to the side of his head.

"Glen, help," the woman spluttered. "He's trying to drown me!"

116

The man lunged and jumped on Ryan's head, holding him under, while the woman kicked and clawed at him with all her might. Ryan cried out, getting a lungful of water as he struggled to get to the surface. But the man held him fast as the woman continued to shriek. *I'm drowning,* Ryan thought desperately.

For a moment Elizabeth's face drifted across his consciousness. "Ryan," her voice whispered. And then there was nothing.

Chapter Seven

"Relax. Try to calm down." Nina took a deep breath in a last-ditch attempt to soothe her nerves. Scanning the beach in an orderly and methodical fashion was practically impossible with her mind raging like this.

Personal concerns are no justification for being inattentive while on duty, she reminded herself darkly. *I can't afford to miss someone in trouble because I'm preoccupied.*

"It's all your fault, Ryan Taylor!" she moaned, leaning back in the big wooden lifeguard chair in Tower 2. "And I don't know what to do about it."

"Hey, Nina!" Jessica strolled by in her red lifeguard suit, her blond ponytail bouncing from the back of her Sweet Valley Shore cap. She leaned against the stilts of Nina's lifeguard chair.

"Congratulations on your promotion. Miranda told me the good news."

Nina looked down, drawing her dark eyebrows into a scowl. "Shouldn't you be at your post?"

Jessica raised her sunglasses. "You look like someone who ate a barrel of lemons. Wasn't this something you wanted?"

Nina glowered. "A ruined summer? Why wouldn't I want that? Maybe I can throw in a case of German measles while I'm at it."

Jessica made a face and crossed her slender arms. "Come on, it can't be that bad."

"Oh yes, it can," Nina shot back, feeling close to tears. She turned her face away and blotted at her eyes with a towel.

Jessica clambered up the ladder and put a calming hand on her arm. "Look, do you want to talk about it?"

I wish I could, Nina thought. Not being able to tell anyone the *whole* reason for her unhappiness at having to take on the head lifeguard job made her feel even worse. But she couldn't bear letting everyone know that she'd broken her vow of a manless summer already.

Nina shrugged and let out a long sigh. "I feel as if my whole summer is blowing up in my face. I had plenty of spare time, and now this." She motioned her arm to indicate the crowded beach dotted with colorful towels, frolicking children, and happy sun worshipers under a brilliant, clear blue sky. At least she could tell her friends half the reason for her unhappiness.

Jessica leaned against the railing and surveyed the beach with a raised eyebrow. "Looks pretty great to me."

Nina groaned. "Sure, in six-hour shifts it's great. But Ryan scheduled himself so that he worked every day, all day. And since he's handing off the responsibility to me, that's what I'll have to do. And I don't want to."

Jessica nodded and brushed aside a strand of her golden blond hair, tucking it back under the bill of her cap. "I see what you mean." She bent down and plucked Nina's suntan lotion from the floor and squirted some on her arms. "Have you tried talking to him?"

Nina shook her head. "I can't even look at him right now. I swear, if we were in the same room, I might take a crack at him."

Giggling, Jessica rubbed the lotion onto her arms, sending the scent of coconut into the salty sea air. "That doesn't sound very encouraging."

"No," Nina agreed. She spied two girls floating toward the jetty on an inner tube and gave two short blasts of her whistle, waving for them to paddle back toward shore.

Jessica slipped off her sunglasses and studied the smudges. She reached for Nina's towel and gave them a quick rub. "What about Liz? Can't she talk some sense into him?"

Nina covered her face with her hands as she thought of her and Elizabeth's blowup earlier in the afternoon. "That's another problem," she mumbled. "Your sister tried to talk to me about Ryan, and I practically bit her head off."

Jessica sighed and slid on her sunglasses. "Hey!" she exclaimed suddenly. "Is that Ryan out there in the water?"

Nina grabbed her binoculars and focused where Jessica was pointing. She could see Ryan bobbing in the water near the sandbar next to a man and a woman. "Looks like they're horsing around," she commented. "He didn't blow his whistle to signal there was any danger."

"Let me see those," Jessica asked, reaching for the binoculars. "Oh, great," she said contemptuously as she adjusted the vision control, "Priya's getting in on the action now, and I can see Ben's not far behind." She handed the binoculars back to Nina.

Nina sighed. Until she figured out a way to get out of being head lifeguard, she'd have to take on the duty of keeping Priya and Jessica separated as well.

Jessica leaned back on the arm of the empty chair. "I wouldn't worry about Liz, Nina. I'm sure she realizes that you're under a lot of pressure with your new position."

121

Nina shrugged and toyed with her whistle. "Maybe, but if neither one of us can get through to Ryan, I don't know what I'm going to do."

Or do I? she thought with a flash. She had the perfect solution right in front of her. "*You* could talk to him, Jess!"

Jessica pulled back, clutching the railing. "I don't know about that."

Nina sat forward in her chair. "Why not? It's perfect. Ryan has no problem with you. You don't have any ulterior motives, so there isn't any reason for him to get defensive with you."

"I know, but . . ."

"All you have to do is talk to him. Tell the truth. Everyone would be happier and better off if he stayed head lifeguard." *Especially me,* Nina thought.

Jessica sighed, twirling her whistle in her hand. "Why should he listen to me?"

"Why shouldn't he?" Nina argued. "Besides, you can convince anyone to do anything," she added sweetly. *A little flattery never hurt,* she thought. Though in Jessica's case the compliment was easy to give. Jessica seemed to have considerable persuasive powers, especially when it came to the weaker sex.

Jessica let the whistle drop and crossed her arms, giving Nina a stern look. "OK, I'll give it a try. But I'm not promising anything."

Nina leaped to her feet, feeling as if a ten-pound weight had suddenly lifted from her shoulders. "Great, Jess," she said, beaming. "I'm sure you'll do your best." Already images of snuggling in Stu's strong arms were dancing in her head.

"Rock-a-bye baby, on the treetop," the young woman sang as she strolled along the boardwalk, carrying a small cooler in one hand and swinging a shopping bag back and forth in the other.

She turned left onto the wooden jetty where the fishermen came in the morning at high tide. As she'd hoped, the pier was now practically deserted. She began walking toward the end of the landing, the ocean wind growing increasingly strong.

"When the wind blows, the cradle will rock." Her voice sounded flat and atonal in the whistling wind. "When the bough breaks, the cradle will fall, and down will come baby, cradle and all."

She let out a shriek of laughter, ignoring the uncomfortable looks of the few die-hard fishermen still hoping for a nibble in the afternoon. When she reached the end of the pier, she leaned over the right side and stared across the water to where Nina was sitting in her lifeguard chair.

123

Oh, Nina dear, do I have a surprise for you, the young woman thought. She watched her rival scan the surging ocean, her beady little eyes roving back and forth from the jetty to the start of the next tower. Chuckling, the young woman crossed over to the other side of the pier—the blind spot in Nina's post.

From her shopping bag she extracted a collapsible fishing rod. She hummed to herself as she put it together. She threaded a thin but extremely strong line through the loops. "Wouldn't want it to break," she said, testing the line once more.

She dug into the pocket of her baggy Windbreaker and pulled out the special hook she'd devised. It was more like a large clamp. This was one piece of bait she didn't want wriggling away.

Now it was time to prepare the line. She looked around, her pulse quickening as a tourist couple in matching Hawaiian shirts started a slow stroll toward the end of the pier where she was standing. If she messed up now, her plan would be foiled.

"Whatcha fishing for?" the man asked, trying to peer into her shopping bag.

The young woman smiled. She knew how to handle nosy intruders. She'd thought ahead. "Eels," she cried, kicking open the cooler with her sneaker and letting one of the slippery, squirming things whip out.

The man jumped back with a cry. He grabbed the woman's arm, and they dashed back to the end of the pier.

The young woman giggled as they fled. *Good,* she thought. *Now I can continue.* She removed her real catch from inside her bag and, with her back turned to the beach, she attached the lure with her makeshift fishing hook.

Slowly, tenderly, she lowered her bait until it bobbed helplessly on the surface of the water. Then she let out more fishing line and smiled as it drifted under the pier, pulled by the ocean's current toward shore and Nina's watchful eyes.

Ryan shot to the surface of the water, gasping for air.

"Ryan! Are you all right?" Priya asked, grabbing onto his arm and propelling him around to her other side.

He winced as salt water stung at the scratches the drowning woman had given him. "I'm fine," he said defensively, shaking Priya off. "Where'd those two people go?"

Disoriented, Ryan looked around, finally realizing he was now standing on the sandbar. The shallow water lapped gently against his heaving chest.

"It's OK, Ryan," Priya said calmly as she treaded water next to him. "I'm going to bring them to shore."

Ryan took a big gulp of air. The man and woman were gripping the side of Priya's rescue board, looking at him warily.

"Grab onto the buoy," Ben ordered, thrusting the red flotation device toward him. "I'll swim you back in."

Ryan pushed it away. "I don't need any help," he barked. "I'm fine."

Ben began to speak, but Ryan ignored him and dove off the sandbar, beginning to swim steadily toward shore. He didn't like Ben and Priya's attitude. So he'd gone under for a moment; big deal. There was nothing in the water he couldn't handle, right?

He shivered as if he'd swum through an icy spot, but the chill came from within. *Who are you kidding?* asked a voice in his head. *That's as close as you've ever come to being fish food.*

Ryan shook his head and continued his even stroke. *It'll never happen,* he thought angrily. *I'm a pro. Pros don't drown.*

Ryan pulled himself out of the ocean, took a few uncertain steps, and sank to his knees on the beach. He banged the side of his head a few times to knock the water out of his ears, but he still felt as if a dizzying fog had wrapped itself around his brain. What had happened with that couple didn't add up.

Ben ran toward him from the water, trailing

the red buoy behind him. "Are you all right?" he asked, squatting at Ryan's side.

"Of course I am," Ryan snapped, despite the weakness he felt in his chest. "Why do you keep asking me that? And you shouldn't drag those things like toys." He pointed to the flotation device.

Ben pulled the buoy up to his side and looked off at the horizon. "I know you weren't planning on working anymore, and it's cool that you tried to make the save. But you didn't look all right out there, man," he said quietly.

Priya jogged up to them. "The couple is going to be OK, but they're a bit shaken up."

Ryan blew some wind from his lips. He still didn't have his breath back. "Why are they shaken up? I rushed out there to save them from drowning and they turned on me like attack dogs." He shook his head. "I'm going to file a formal complaint. Have them banned from the beach." He began struggling to his feet.

But Ben's forceful hand on his shoulder held him down. "I don't think that would be a good idea."

"Why?" Ryan argued. "Who needs menaces like them around?"

Ben and Priya exchanged glances. "They said they weren't having any problems until you came and . . . um . . ."

"What?"

Ben scratched the back of his neck uneasily. "They say you tried to drown them."

Ryan's mouth dropped open. "What are you talking about? They were flailing around out there. They'd probably be dead if it weren't for me."

"They were only fooling around," Priya said quietly, looking down at him. "If you weren't sure, you should have blown your whistle and signaled to them . . . and us. That's what you taught us to do. We *thought* you weren't on duty anymore."

Ryan narrowed his eyes and scowled. "I was afraid it would be too late."

"Where's your whistle?" Ben asked.

Ryan looked down at his bare, heaving chest. It was dimpled with goose bumps. *Whistle?* he thought. He didn't have the slightest idea. He glared at the two of them. "What's with the twenty questions?" he roared. "They were drowning. I saw it!"

Ben stood up next to Priya and spread his hands. "There's a lot of glare today. Anybody could have made that mistake."

Ryan jumped to his feet, ignoring the spinning sensation in his head. "I didn't make a mistake!" he shouted. "They were in trouble. And no one saw it but me. So if they—or you—don't like it, then next time you can all come floating in on the tide—blue and waterlogged!"

"Ryan!" Priya cried.

But Ryan ignored her, stomping off in the direction of the main tower. *People are too uptight around here,* he thought, glowering. *And I'm sick of it. I saved those people from drowning, and I don't care what anybody else thinks. Now I know I'm doing the right thing.*

Nina jumped to her feet, her hands shaking, her heart pounding. "Oh, my gosh!" she whispered violently. There was a baby floating in the water just under the pier! The child was bobbing faceup, wisps of blond-white hair trailing out from around a bright red bonnet.

Nina blew three long blasts on her whistle—SOS—and leaped down from the tower. She streaked across the sand and dove into the water, plowing through the surf, her strong, slender arms stroking through the waves at breakneck speed. She had to get to the child before it was too late—she just had to.

But how? she wondered despairingly. The currents around the piers were notoriously dangerous. Buoy lines had been set up establishing a ten-yard no-swim zone around them. If a swimmer even got close to the roped-off area, Nina always made a point of emphatically signaling them away.

"How could I have been so blind?" she cried, frantically streaking through the water. Obviously she had failed to notice that anyone had strayed into the forbidden area. But a child? "Of all the times to mess up," she sobbed. "A baby's life is at stake!"

Nina bit down hard on her lip to keep her concentration. She could feel her body surging with adrenaline, inches away from hysteria. A child was in trouble, and it was her fault! How could she ever learn to live with that?

And where are the baby's parents? her mind screamed. *Had they already drowned? Been carried out to sea to be washed up onto the beach when the ocean was through with them?* Nina gasped and continued her fierce stroke. She would save that child. "Hold on," she grunted, "I'm coming!"

She was fast approaching the base of the pylons where she'd seen the baby. Now the currents swirled in every direction. The closer she got to the foaming eddies, the more they pushed and pulled at her body, threatening to drag her into a grinding whirlpool. Nina gasped for breath, paddling furiously to keep above the churning white water, desperately searching for any sight of the bright red bonnet.

Her body exhausted and battered, she finally managed to grab hold of one of the pylons.

Somehow her foot found a small piece of wood that was nailed to it, and she hoisted herself up above the water, squinting as she scanned the area for any sign of the baby. Suddenly two rogue waves crashed together around the pylon, nearly throwing her back into the roaring water. She hung on with all her might, still seeing nothing.

The baby's underwater! her brain shouted. The sudden image of a child's drowned body, limp and lifeless, made her cry out in fright. Nina took a huge gulp of air and threw herself off the precarious safety of the pylon and into the tumultuous water below, ignoring the stinging salt water in her eyes as she searched the violent ocean floor.

She felt with her hands through the murky weeds that grew up around the poles, stifling a cry as a jagged edge sliced her fingers. A sob struggled in her throat as she came up for air with no baby in her arms.

"Where are you?" she cried, panic and horror ripping through her. Again she dove under, keeping herself down much longer than she should have, her lungs screaming from the sustained punishment. But still she pushed herself, searching and praying that somehow the body she would find would still have life in it. *Please!* she begged. *Don't let that baby die!*

Chapter Eight

"This is scary, Winston," Wendy cried. "Are you sure you know where you're going?"

Winston gulped silently and looked around. The woman on the phone had said they should go to Seagull Lane off Beach Boulevard. But this was Seagull Lane, and all he saw was a deserted alley full of boarded-up shops. "It's just down here," he replied hopefully.

Wendy grabbed the back of his white polo shirt. "We've already passed that Dumpster twice, Winston. I think we'd better get out of here—and *fast*."

Winston grimaced. He was beginning to think Wendy was right. Even in daylight this place was creepy. They'd seen more than a couple of shady-looking characters in the past few minutes. But he hated to give up. After all, the ad in the paper had sounded promising: Madame Yphantides, Chakra Therapist—Will Transform Your Energy, Leading to a Calm, Centered Clarity. It was exactly what Wendy needed.

"OK. Hold on a second," Winston said, stalling for time. He scanned the facades of the derelict buildings once again. Surely there would be a sign in the window. *Nothing*. And it was becoming increasingly clear that they'd better get out of there before something happened that would be detrimental to the whole healing-process thing.

Winston turned around and headed for a slit in the wire fencing at the end of the alleyway. "I think that's the hole we climbed through to get in here," he murmured nervously. They were halfway there when, out of nowhere, a gnarled hand, its fingers heavily decorated with elaborately jeweled rings, shot out and clutched his arm.

"Yeow!" Winston cried, pulling back in fright.

A woman smiled back at him. She wore a colorful head scarf, and her eyelids were heavy with turquoise shadow. "Mr. Egbert?" she inquired. Her voice was deep, with a slightly Mediterranean lilt.

"I know that voice!" Winston exclaimed. "You're—"

"Madame Yphantides, at your service. Please accompany me."

Winston turned to Wendy, who was cowering behind him. "OK, Wendy?"

She furrowed her brow, feigning fright, and nodded.

They followed Madame Yphantides through a large gray door halfway down the alley. *I never would have found* this *place,* Winston thought as she led them around a series of darkened passageways. Finally they came out into a small, cluttered room filled with burning candles. The afternoon light was blocked out by heavy black curtains.

Madame Yphantides smiled. "Take a seat, Mr. Egbert. Wendy, you may lie on the platform." She indicated a long, flat cushion covered with red damask.

"How did you know my name?" Wendy gasped.

"Yeah!" Winston swallowed, his eyes huge. "How *did* you?" Maybe this Madame Yphantides really *was* a mystic.

Madame Yphantides laughed. "I'm not a fortune-teller. I heard Mr. Egbert call you by name."

"Oh." Winston nodded, relieved. "Duh. Of course."

Wendy tucked her pleated blue skirt under her legs and lay down on the red platform. Winston sank into an overstuffed blue chair close by.

Madame Yphantides knelt on Wendy's other side. "Mr. Egbert has told me your love chakra is blocked. This is primarily due to your holding on to negative karma from previous lives. With your help I will perform a karmic matrix removal."

Wendy giggled. "Is that sort of like spring cleaning?"

Madame Yphantides raised one penciled-in eyebrow. "Exactly." She turned to Winston. "Mr. Egbert, light the candles by Wendy's head, please."

Winston picked up Madame Yphantides's ornate, gold-plated cigarette lighter and fumbled with it until he finally got a flame. He lit the row of ivory-colored candles, trying to keep his hands from shaking. "Anything else?"

Madame Yphantides pressed her fingers into a steeple shape. "My onyx box."

Winston looked behind him, spied the box, and handed it to the healer.

"Now you may rest, Mr. Egbert. And Wendy, our work shall begin." Madame Yphantides pulled out a crystal of rose quartz from her box and placed it on Wendy's blue-flowered blouse, over her heart. "Root, navel, stomach, heart, throat, brow, crown. Chakra, chakra, round and round." She chanted faster and faster until the sounds became a blur. At the same time she made movements as if she were pulling invisible energy from Wendy's chest.

Winston watched in alarm as the corners of Wendy's smiling mouth began to turn downward and her dancing gray eyes filled with tears. "Oh, my gosh," she sobbed.

Winston dove to his knees before her, grabbing her hand. "What's wrong?"

Wendy squeezed her eyes tight.

Madame Yphantides continued to chant, though she had stopped making pulling motions.

"It's Pedro, isn't it?" Winston prodded. "You're not ready to give him up. Come on, Wendy, you can tell me."

Wendy sat up abruptly. The crystal rolled to the floor. "No," she insisted. "I *was* thinking about him. But I *am* ready." She wiped the tears from her face with her sleeve. "He's history. Just a leftover connection from a past life."

Madame Yphantides retrieved the quartz. "Wendy, please, lie back down. We are not finished yet."

Wendy staggered to her feet. "No, I am. I've seen enough. Pedro and I are through."

Winston looked over at Madame Yphantides helplessly. *That can't be right,* he thought.

The healer shook her head. "There's more work to do, Wendy."

Wendy ignored her, pushing past them and starting down the dark passageway toward the door.

"Madame Yphantides!" Winston cried. "What should I do?"

"Go after her, Mr. Egbert," the healer advised.

"Your friend needs your help. She has not yet fully answered the question that brought you here."

"OK. I'll do everything I can," Winston vowed. It was obvious that Wendy still felt something for Pedro. And it was up to Winston to prove it before it was too late.

Nina rocked back and forth on the beach. "She's still out there," she sobbed. "We've got to find her."

Ben had wrapped a heavy blanket around her shuddering shoulders and briskly rubbed her arms. "Shhh, Nina," he whispered soothingly. "The Coast Guard will find her."

Nina shook her head, tears streaming down her cheeks. "It's all my fault. I should have seen her playing along the pier. I never should have let her get so close to the water."

"But you didn't see her," Ben murmured. "No one saw her."

"Then I should have saved her," Nina cried. "But she was out too far. How did she get out so far? How?"

"Nina," Ben said quietly. "Are you sure you saw a baby?"

Nina looked up at him in confusion. "What are you saying? Of course I saw a baby. She's still out there."

Theo squatted down on her other side.

"Nina, the Coast Guard hasn't found her. And they think the chances are very slim that they could have missed her. They're coming back in."

"What?" Nina gasped. "That's crazy! How can they just leave that baby out there?" She threw off the blanket and started to get up. She would go out again. She would find the child.

"Nina, stop it," Ben scolded. "You're not going anywhere but home. Look at you—you're exhausted. You could have drowned out there."

"But I didn't," Nina snapped. "A child did. The least I can do for her parents is recover her body." She dropped her head in her hands as grief overtook her. Sobs racked her slender frame.

Ben replaced the blanket around her. "I'm taking you home."

Nina felt herself being lifted up and walked toward the beach house. She felt as if she were outside her own body, as if she had no control or will of her own.

"She's still out there, Ben," she moaned. "We've got to find her."

"We will, Nina, we will," he murmured. "If she's out there."

Nina stopped in her tracks and looked up at him through puffy, sore eyes. "What do you mean, *if?*"

Ben removed his baseball cap and ran a hand through his dark hair. "Nina, the Coast Guard searched for over an hour and found nothing. They're positive that the way the tides are running, there's no way that a body, especially a child's, wouldn't have been washed back onshore. You must have felt how hard it was to swim out there. Imagine a child—she would have been thrown back in seconds."

Nina shook her head. "Then why wasn't she on the beach?"

Ben sighed. "Why weren't her parents?"

Nina turned away, swallowing hard. "Drowned too."

"No," Ben stated. "They definitely would have been spotted." He cleared his throat. "Nina, are you sure what you saw was a child? Are you sure it wasn't something else? Maybe a piece of debris?"

Nina's mouth dropped open, and for a moment she was speechless. She'd never heard anything so absurd. "With blond hair and a bright red bonnet?" she roared. "If you're trying to make me feel better, this is *not* how you do it. It's bad enough I couldn't find her without you trying to deny her whole existence." She threw the blanket to the sandy ground.

Ben picked it up and put it around her again. "Nina, please, you could go into shock."

"No!" she screamed, pulling away from him. "Leave me alone."

She ran for the beach house, hot, bitter tears filling her already swollen eyes. She was going to have to live with this for the rest of her life. At least she could have some support in her pain. *But no,* she thought bitterly. *I'm going to be left to mourn alone.* She raced up to her bedroom, taking the steps two at a time. All she wanted to do was collapse onto her bed.

But as Nina flung open the bedroom door she felt her screams being almost physically ripped from her lungs. Staring back at her from the bed—neatly propped up on her pillows— was the "baby" she'd nearly died trying to save.

Its eyes were wide open, staring vacantly from their sockets, and its white hair was matted beneath a soggy red bonnet. Seaweed trailed from its inert limbs. *Plastic limbs.*

"A doll!" Nina gasped, beginning to shake uncontrollably. She charged to the bed and grabbed the doll. "Who would do this?" Nina demanded as if the doll could answer her. "And why? Why! *Why!*"

The young woman collapsed onto the sand, her body convulsing with laughter as Nina's screams rang out over the seashore. She only wished she'd been able to stay there, hidden in Nina's closet, to see her expression when she came face-to-face with baby "Matilda."

She wiped the tears of glee from her eyes with the hem of her T-shirt and stood up. "Poor little lamb," she tittered. "I hope your new mommy has time to take care of you."

Before I take care of her, she thought menacingly before disappearing into the dunes.

Jessica stood up and stretched her arms on her post at Tower 4. The sun was starting its slow descent over the horizon. The last of the beachgoers were packing away their picnics and shaking out their sandy towels. The ocean breeze had picked up speed and was adding a chill to the air—another day of lifeguarding was coming to an end. From the chair next to her Miranda let out a long yawn.

"Whew, that last save really took it out of me," Jessica joked. "It's a good thing our shifts are over."

Miranda giggled, tossing back a lock of her dark brown hair. "Right. That was some *save*, Jessica. The water wasn't even up to that guy's abs."

"But what abs!" Jessica wiggled her eyebrows up and down. "And anyway, I haven't had a date this *whole* summer."

"Whole summer? It hasn't even been a week, Jess."

"Well, I thought the least he could do was ask me out after my dramatic rescue attempt."

Miranda rolled her eyes. "Next time make

sure your drowning victim doesn't have a girl-friend before you 'plunge in,' shall we say?"

Jessica sighed and gathered up her beach towel and tote. "I know, I usually leap before I look. That's the story of my life. But I don't think there *are* any single guys left in Sweet Valley Shore."

Miranda untied her lifeguard jacket from around her waist and slipped it on. "There're plenty. Walking down the boardwalk this morning, I got asked out twice. Neither one was really my type, though."

Jessica groaned and tossed her empty water bottle into her tote. "I must be cursed. No one notices me anymore. I could use some real help in the love department."

Miranda snorted. "What you need is to stop chasing after other people's boyfriends."

Jessica straightened up, her aquamarine eyes flashing. "If you're referring to Ben, he was *my* boyfriend first."

Miranda gave Jessica a rueful look. "*Was* being the operative word." She pulled on her black sweatpants. "And anyway, why waste your time on someone who's been acting like a first-class loser? And, I might add, who's obviously not interested? You need a guy who wants *you*. Who appreciates what the amazing Jessica Wakefield has to offer."

Jessica sighed again. Miranda had a point. Why *was* she wasting her time trying to get back with Ben? "You're right, Miranda. From now on I'm only interested in guys who are interested in me. No more chasing after the guys who aren't."

"Go, girlfriend!" Miranda cheered. "That's the attitude." She climbed down the ladder after Jessica. "Tell you what. How about a girls' night out tomorrow? A few of my friends from Bard are in town, and we're going to hit some clubs. Want to come? Many men!" she finished tantalizingly.

"OK," Jessica agreed. "I'll do it. From here on in, my luck is changing. I can feel it."

"That's the spirit. Now how about coming with me for a run? It's a great way to meet guys. *Available* guys, that is."

Jessica was sorely tempted. *But I can't,* she thought. *I promised Nina I'd have a chat with Ryan.* "I'll save my charms for tomorrow night," she offered. "But if you see a really cute one, hold on to him for me."

"Sorry." Miranda laughed as she began jogging toward the boardwalk. "If he's cute, he's all mine."

Jessica waved good-bye, her smile wide and sunny. But as soon as Miranda's back was turned, her shoulders slumped and her face was overcome with gloom. *Figures,* she thought as she sulked over to the main tower. *The way this summer's going, I'll be lucky if I get one kiss!*

Jessica shook out her hair and tried to brighten her mood as she entered the main tower. *"You get more with honey than vinegar,"* her mother always said. And if she was going to try to convince Ryan to stay on as head lifeguard, she'd better at least try and act upbeat. Steeling herself with a deep breath, she tapped on the door to his living quarters. "Ryan?"

"Back here," she heard him call from inside.

Jessica pushed open the door to Ryan's room and immediately felt the blood rush to her face. The blinds were drawn, and the only light was from a lamp whose shade had been covered by a piece of blue silk material. Ryan was lying across his bed, his tanned, muscular body bare except for a skimpy square-cut bathing suit. In the dim light his body glowed like a Greek god's.

For the second time in as many days Jessica felt the crush she'd once had on Ryan resurge. Sure, she'd put his flirtatious behavior of the previous morning out of her mind, but now she found herself fidgeting as his sensuous lips broke into a knowing grin.

"Jessica," he exclaimed, sitting up. "What a surprise. Come on in. I'm glad to see you."

Jessica stumbled into the small room, her eyes glued to Ryan's powerful swimmer's physique.

"I'm glad to see you too," she managed, falling squarely onto a rickety wooden stool a few feet from his bed. She widened her eyes in mock astonishment. "And so much of you."

Ryan threw back his head and laughed. "That's what I love about you, Jessica—you're always quick." He lay back on his bed, stretching his hands behind his head, his biceps flexing. "You obviously know how to have a good time."

Jessica ran a slender hand through her long blond hair and gave him a sly look. "Fun's my middle name."

Ryan patted the checkered bedspread beside him. "Wouldn't you be more comfortable sitting here?"

Jessica gulped. *I'll say,* she thought, slipping her hands, palms down, beneath her thighs and sitting on them. *But I have a feeling I'll get in a lot less trouble if I stay over here.* "Thanks, but I wouldn't want to get your bed all sandy," she said coyly.

Ryan smiled and moistened his lips. The impact of that seemingly small gesture made her suddenly, anxiously aware that she had on her red swimsuit and not much else. Outside in the daylight it was simply her work uniform, but right now she couldn't help noticing how Ryan was letting his eyes travel along her curves.

And why shouldn't he? she thought defensively,

trying to push away the twinge of guilt she felt at being checked out by her sister's boyfriend. She'd always prided herself on her appearance, hadn't she? It wasn't her fault if Ryan found her attractive.

"I don't care about the sand," Ryan said huskily, his golden brown eyes twinkling. "But you're welcome to use the shower if you'd like to clean off." He pointed to the door off the bedroom.

Jessica giggled, hoping she didn't sound as nervous as she felt. "Then my suit would be all wet. I didn't bring a change of clothes."

Ryan jumped up, pulling open the middle drawer of his dresser. "Would this do?" He held up one of his own white, extra-large T-shirts. On Jessica it would make a short and very sexy dress.

Jessica raised an eyebrow, her lips curling into a grin. She was beginning to enjoy this. It was about time someone paid attention to her. Someone gorgeous and sexy and—

Not your twin's boyfriend! a small voice in her head added. Wasn't this exactly what she and Miranda had been taking about earlier? No matter how badly Jessica was aching for recognition, Ryan Taylor was strictly off-limits. And because he was dating her twin, he was *beyond* off-limits.

Jessica stifled a groan. "I'll have to take a rain check. What I really wanted to talk to you about was Nina and the head lifeguard post. What's the deal?"

Ryan covered his head with the T-shirt. "I don't want to talk about it," he muttered, throwing the shirt aside and dropping back down on his bed. "That's a bore. It's a beautiful evening. Why don't you come over here? We can talk about nothing at all." He patted the bed again. "Wet or sandy, I don't care."

Jessica felt her heart do a double flip. Girlfriend or no girlfriend, sister or no sister, Ryan's actions were practically shouting that he was available. She slowly stood up, her blue-green eyes locked with his. She took a step toward him.

Wait a minute! her mind cautioned. Even if Ryan's flirting was wholeheartedly innocent, she knew that going anywhere near him would only spell trouble. Elizabeth was crazy about Ryan. If she only knew how he was acting right now—it would kill her! *Better get out of this one, Jess, and fast,* she told herself.

"I—I've got to go," she said quickly.

"Don't."

Jessica shrugged helplessly and took two steps back until she reached the door. Then regretfully, with a last teasing smile, she slipped out, running down the wooden path before she could change her mind.

Chapter
Nine

"Oh, Stu," Nina whispered as she pedaled hurriedly over the bridge leading to Stu's adobe beach house. "I need you right now. All I want to do is be in your arms."

The setting sun lit up the sky in a riotous blanket of purples and pinks. On any other night Nina would have been overwhelmed by its beauty. But right now all she felt was overwhelmed. *Stu will comfort me,* she assured herself. *Stu will make it all right.*

She hoped he wouldn't mind her showing up without warning. *But this has been the most horrible day of my life,* she thought. *First I had the head lifeguard job practically forced on me and then—* Suddenly the image of the plastic doll being tossed about by the ocean's raging water flashed through her mind. She shuddered, biting back tears as she maneuvered her mountain bike off the bridge and onto SeaMist Island.

"Who would deliberately make it look like a baby was drowning?" she cried out, almost losing control of the bike. She steadied herself and continued cycling.

After the initial fright of finding the doll in her room had worn off, she'd felt a huge sense of relief. At least she knew that no one, let alone a little baby, had drowned on her shift. But her relief was slowly turning into a new kind of anxiety. "Why was the doll put in *my* room?" she wondered aloud.

Ben and Theo thought the doll had been left there to put her mind at ease. That the prankster from the beach had felt guilty that the joke had gone too far. But Nina wasn't so sure. Her mind quickly flashed to the memory of her ripped swimsuits, of her falling unconscious, and of the hard push she'd been given at the fire-walking ceremony.

Someone's out to get me, she thought, shuddering. *But who? And why?*

She tried to keep calm as she pedaled up the long, winding driveway to Stu's place, but she was well aware that her legs were pumping almost frantically. What she needed now was to collapse and let someone take care of her for a change. Stu did that better than anyone she'd ever met.

She coasted up to the dusty red exterior and dismounted, feeling relieved and almost instantly calmer. *Stu will make things better,* Nina thought. *He always does.*

She jumped off her bike and leaned it against a palm tree. The gentle sound of the lapping waves just over the dunes made her calmer still. She could see Stu inside, through the huge sliding glass doors that opened into the spacious living area.

Stu had designed both the house and the streamlined, Eastern-style furnishings that sparsely decorated each room. The living room had been arranged based on feng shui principles and echoed Stu's desire for beauty and simplicity. Natural wood floors were set off by a long, low, white-cushioned couch and a simple wooden table based on the Tibetan prayer cabinets that Stu had showed her in a magazine article. A large, open fireplace took up one side of the room.

Stu sat cross-legged on his meditation chair—a high-backed teakwood platform—which stood opposite the couch, angled slightly away from the sliding doors. He was reading, his handsome brow furrowed in concentration.

Nina felt her heart swell. With all the confusion swirling around her, Stu was like the very island he lived on. How appropriate that he'd literally rescued her from the sea. He was the one person she could trust right now. He was completely different from all the other men she'd ever known. He didn't play games with her feelings. He cherished her.

Nina stepped onto the porch and walked silently through the open doors into the house. "Stu," she whispered, bending down and wrapping her arms around him from behind the teakwood chair. He yelped and leaped to his feet, practically knocking Nina over backward.

"Stu, I'm sorry!" Nina cried. "I didn't mean to startle you." She stepped away, unnerved by Stu's outburst. It wasn't like him at all.

"It's OK." He laughed in what seemed to be relief. "It's nothing. I was just . . ." He ran his left hand across his forehead as he surreptitiously slipped the paper he was reading into the back pocket of his jeans with his right. "You kind of took me by surprise."

Nina frowned. Something was up. "What was that?" she asked in a casual tone.

"What?" Stu asked innocently, proffering both hands.

Nina walked around the chair, trying to look behind him. But as she moved so did he, keeping his back away from her. "That piece of paper. I saw you reading it from the door."

Stu shrugged and backed into the middle of the living room. His normally placid demeanor was nowhere to be seen. "It's . . . it's nothing," he stammered, laughing once nervously. "So . . . ," he started. "How're you doing? I wasn't expecting you to cruise by tonight. I was—"

"If it's nothing, why are you hiding it from me?" Nina's eyes narrowed suspiciously, stopping him in midsentence. In spite of her corded cotton sweater she felt a chill run through her, and she knew it had nothing to do with the cool night air.

Stu groaned and leaned against the mantel of his fireplace. "You don't want to know."

Nina felt the blood start to pound in her temples. Stu's house was the one place she'd thought she could feel safe. But now, even here, she was feeling unsure. "Just tell me. I've had the worst day imaginable. I can't take any more of this."

Stu's bright blue eyes shone with compassion. "Let me make you a hot cup of herbal tea. I'll stoke up the fire and we can mellow out while you tell me about your day."

"Stu!" Nina spat. "Don't change the subject, please, I'm begging you. What are you hiding from me?"

"It would be better if you didn't ask."

"If you're going to keep things from me, we're finished," Nina shouted, storming across the room. She held out her hand, her dark eyes blazing. There was no way she was going to let doubt and confusion enter yet another part of her life. If Stu couldn't be straight with her, she was leaving.

Stu reluctantly pulled the paper from his pocket and handed it to her. He sighed resignedly as she began to unfold the handwritten letter. "Don't say I didn't warn you."

Nina felt the color drain from her face as she scanned the page. *Dearest Stuart . . . I haven't forgotten you . . . beautiful times . . . should never have strayed from your side . . . our true love . . . waking beside you . . . bodies pressed close . . . seeing you yesterday . . .*

"What is this?" she gasped, the words stinging her eyes. "This—this is a love letter!" Her body began to shake. "You've got someone else!" Her heart felt as if it had been crushed and thrown to the ground. How could she have been so wrong about him?

"No, Nina," Stu cried. "Let me explain." He moved toward her, arms outstretched. But Nina pushed him away.

"The explanation is right here," she sobbed, waving the piece of paper in front of him. "You've been using me!"

"I would never use you, mermaid," Stu pleaded. "I love you."

She flung the letter to the hardwood floor and ran for the open door. "Well, I hate you,

Stu Kirkwood," she screamed. "I thought you were different. But you're just like *all* men. You're nothing but a worthless dog!"

"Winston, I don't know what to do," Elizabeth mumbled, holding up the hem of her long, flowing skirt so she could dip her toes into the cool ocean water.

Winston jumped back as the surf licked at the soles of his sneakers. "I presume you're talking about Ryan again."

Elizabeth blushed and pulled her loose hair back into a ponytail. "Sorry . . . I guess I'm not very good company tonight. It's just that I can't seem to stop thinking about him. He's got me worried."

Winston sighed. "It's OK. I'm pretty preoccupied with Wendy. I took her to a chakra healer this afternoon, hoping she would help sort out Wendy's feelings for Pedro."

Elizabeth raised an eyebrow and looked at him skeptically. "Did it do any good?"

Winston shook his head. "Wendy insisted on leaving before Madame Yphantides could finish the healing process. But I'm sure she still loves Pedro. I don't believe she could have fallen out of love with him so fast."

Elizabeth nodded. "Only my sister has that rare talent for falling in and out of love at the drop of a hat. And even *she* seems to be having her share of trouble getting over Ben."

It's definitely not something I can do, she thought, her feelings for Ryan flowing over her like a wave.

"I just don't know what to do," Winston said, picking up a rock and skimming it across the surface of the water. It skipped twice before being swallowed up by a wave. "I know she still feels something for Pedro, but she won't tell me about it."

"Well, has Wendy told *Pedro* how she's feeling, at least?"

Winston zipped up his Windbreaker as they turned and walked up the beach. "Pedro's tour has moved to eastern Europe, and Wendy hasn't been able to reach him. To be honest, I don't think she's tried too hard."

Elizabeth dropped to the ground and began to brush the sand from her bare feet. "She probably wouldn't know what to say to him even if she *could* find him. It's hard to know what to say to someone when you don't know how they'll respond."

"Like Ryan?"

Elizabeth pulled on her sandals. "Exactly. All evening I've been rehearsing what I'm going to say to him and how I'm going to say it. Like, do I burst in and demand to know what's going on? Or should I ask to be invited in and sweetly offer to listen if there's anything he wants to get off his chest?" She looked up at Winston, hoping to read answers on his face. She found only sympathy. "Either way, I know he'll shut me out."

Winston offered her a hand up. "Sometimes you need to put your feelings aside."

Elizabeth wiped the sand from her skirt. "What do you mean?"

"Sometimes you need to be strong for the other person. To help them over whatever it is that's bothering them, even if they think they don't need your help."

Elizabeth cocked her head, studying him intently. "Go on."

"Take Ryan. He's obviously going through something. Every time you try to talk to him, he lashes out. But if you run away, you two will never work it out."

"But that's not my fault!" Elizabeth cried. "He's chasing me away."

Winston shook his head and smiled sadly. "You've got to be tough. Love's about being there for the other person when they're down."

Elizabeth sighed and stared out at the shimmering sun as it began to disappear beneath the edge of the horizon. "So what you're saying is, I should try again and not take no for an answer."

"If you want another go at this relationship."

Elizabeth jumped and clapped. "Winston, you're a genius. As soon as we finish our walk

I'm going to find him and get everything out in the open." She turned on her heels, determined to run as quickly as she could to Ryan's place.

Winston laughed and grabbed her arm, spinning her around. "I think your subconscious is way ahead of you." He pointed to the squat building in front of them. They were practically in the main tower's shadow already.

Elizabeth laughed. "I didn't realize . . . I mean, we can finish our walk."

Winston grinned. "Don't stall. And don't worry about it, OK? Everything will be fine. I'll catch you tomorrow."

"Thanks, Winston." She kissed him on the cheek. "Someday when you're having relationship problems, I promise I'll listen to you. No matter how much you drone on!"

"I'll remember that." Winston laughed, turning away and starting back to the boardwalk. "Good luck."

Elizabeth waved good-bye and took a deep breath before walking up the wooden stairs and pushing open the door. Inside the main tower there was nothing but total darkness. She stumbled through, feeling her way with her hands until she reached the door to Ryan's living quarters.

"Ryan?" she called softly.

A gruff voice answered her back. "Come in."

Elizabeth slipped through the door and

gasped. Ryan was sitting at his table, a bottle of whiskey in one hand and a glass in the other.

"Ryan, don't do it!" she cried. "You can get through this without drinking! Don't take that first sip!"

Ryan turned to face her, his features twisted and contorted. "You're too late," he slurred, downing the glass of whiskey in two long gulps. He threw back his head as a wild howl shook his body.

Elizabeth instinctively moved toward him, arms outstretched. But as his bloodshot eyes locked with hers, she gasped and stumbled backward at what she saw in them. Ryan's chilling howl hadn't been a cry for help. It had been cruel, mocking laughter aimed directly at her.

"Nina, wait!" Stu shouted, grabbing hold of her sweater as she tearfully fought to free her bicycle from the long grass beside his porch.

Nina whirled around, wrenching her arm from his grip. She compressed her lips tightly, trying to keep the angry, hurt tears from spilling from her eyes. "How could you, Stu?"

"Please, Nina," he whispered, holding his hands out toward her. "I haven't done anything to deceive you. I swear. Since I've met you, my whole life has changed. You're the only woman I've truly loved."

Nina took a step back and crossed her arms.

More than anything in the world she wanted to believe him. *But how can I?* she wondered. *I can't—not when that letter says he's deceived me.*

"Please, Nina, I'd do anything for you. You know that."

Nina paused. "Then explain that letter. I want to know everything."

Stu sighed loudly. "If you come back inside, I'll tell you."

"OK." She nodded, following him into the living room and collapsing into the teakwood meditation chair opposite Stu's white-cushioned couch.

"I'm sorry I was trying to hide the letter," he apologized. "That was wrong, and I know it. I don't want us to have any secrets from each other."

"Fair enough."

Stu bent down and picked up the letter from where Nina had flung it on the floor. "Three months ago I went to Changes. You know, the club near the boardwalk?"

Nina nodded.

"I met a girl there. We started dancing. Her name was Rachel."

Rachel? Nina bolted upright in her chair. "Not Rachel Max?" she asked, stunned. Rachel Max had been head lifeguard of the South Beach Squad last summer—the sworn rivals of the Sweet Valley Shore lifeguards. She was a tall, sultry, gorgeous brunette, but definitely not a nice person. In fact, she was the last girl Nina could picture with Stu. "With long dark hair?"

Stu dropped down onto the couch and shook his head. "This girl had short blond hair." He grimaced in discomfort. "And I never did learn her last name."

Nina frowned. "How long were you seeing her?"

"That's the point," Stu said, getting up and beginning to pace the floor in front of the fireplace. "It was just a one-night thing."

Nina felt her stomach give a lurch. "One-night *thing*? Or do you mean a one-night *stand*, Stu?" He shrugged uncomfortably. "Did you have sex with this woman?"

Stu turned and faced Nina squarely. "I know it was stupid . . . I should never have slept with her. But—"

"But what?" Nina asked. Her mouth felt dry, and her hands were shaking. She flattened them on the armrests of the chair.

Stu let out a deep breath and twisted the hem of his T-shirt. "It was aeons since I'd met anyone I even liked. Rachel seemed different . . . you know . . . cool. I didn't think it was going to be a one-night stand. I thought . . . I don't know . . . that there was a spark between us."

Nina fidgeted in her chair. This was one of the hardest things she'd ever had to listen to.

Even harder than hearing another woman pick up her boyfriend's phone. She was desperately trying to keep an open mind. Nina knew all too well that both men *and* women sometimes made mistakes of character. But the thought of Stu jumping into bed with a near-total stranger . . .

I have to stay in the present, she advised herself. *I need to listen to what he has to say now.*

Stu dropped his gaze to the beige throw rug in front of the fireplace and smoothed it down with his foot. "But the next morning," he went on, "she started acting weird." He looked up at Nina, his soft blue eyes begging her to understand. "When I woke up, she'd rearranged the furniture in here. My meditation chair was over there." He pointed to the wall beside the door. "The couch was over here." He shook his head. "She was talking about painting the kitchen a different color, as if this were her house too. It freaked me out majorly."

Nina could see it was as difficult for Stu to talk about the one-night stand as it was for her to hear about it. But they had to get it out in the open. All of it. "Then what happened?" she prompted uneasily.

Stu sat back on the sofa and ran a hand through his tousled hair. "I guess I played the coward. I bailed out of here and went to visit my brother for a month on his ranch in

Montana. I'd only been back a few weeks when I met you. She must have seen me in town and realized I was back."

Nina felt anger flare up inside her. It was one thing to make an error of judgment, but trying to sneak out of it was another thing entirely. "So she thinks you two are still going out?"

"No!" Stu said, grabbing a large brocade cushion and holding it against his chest. "She can't. I made it clear we weren't right for each other."

"How? By pulling a disappearing act?"

Stu shook his head. "It was more than that. What did you expect me to do? I didn't want to be harsh on her, not with her acting so weird. I wanted to let her down easy."

Nina rose to her feet. "You mean let yourself off easy by lying to her. Which means you could be lying to me too."

Stu jumped up. "That's not true. I've never lied to you."

Nina's eyes blazed. "Sins of omission are just as bad, Stu. You didn't want me to see that letter. How do I know there isn't more to this? That letter says she saw you yesterday."

"That's a lie," Stu cried. "I saw her that one time, and that was it."

Nina grimaced and held up her hands. "I can't handle this right now. I thought I could trust you, but now I'm not sure."

Stu looked at her, his blue eyes wide with despair. "I didn't mean to do anything wrong," he whispered. "I'm sorry if I've hurt you. It's the last thing I would ever want to do. Please, Nina, stay with me."

Nina shook her head sadly and willed herself to walk away. "I can't," she mumbled. "This is too much for me. I've had enough drama this week. I can't handle any more." She turned away from him and walked out into the clear, cool night.

Ryan had to grip the edges of the table to keep from falling over. He couldn't help it. The sight of poor, long-suffering Elizabeth, her sensitive little face scrunched up in concern, was too hilarious. He knew it should have been sad, but instead it seemed hysterically funny. "Where were you two days ago, Elizabeth?" he roared. "You're a little late now!"

He watched as the color drained from Elizabeth's face and her eyes widened into two round disks. "You're drunk!" she gasped, slumping against the wall.

Elizabeth's dramatic cry set off a fresh round of laughter that Ryan could hardly take. He felt as if his stomach would rupture. "Stop it!" he croaked, tears streaming down his cheeks. "You're killing me!"

"Ryan, you've got to get hold of yourself!" Elizabeth screeched, making a grab for the whiskey.

Ryan quickly snatched both the bottle and glass from her reach and set them down behind him. Some of the liquor had splattered on his hand, and he wiped it off on the front of his polo shirt.

"You'll have to be quicker than that," he snarled, irritation replacing his amusement at Elizabeth's concern. He felt his lip curl into a mocking sneer. "You see, Liz, it's all about hand-eye coordination," he said gravely. He brought the glass to his lips and gulped down a big swallow of whiskey. "See? Nothing to it." He slammed the glass back onto the table and reached behind him for the bottle.

Elizabeth shook her head, her bottom lip trembling. "How can you do this to yourself? Can't you see it's wrong?"

Ryan snorted and twisted off the top of the whiskey bottle. "*Wrong*, Elizabeth? Since when is having fun wrong? So I have a little to drink . . . so what? Everyone else does it."

Elizabeth wrapped her arms around herself and stared down at him, brow furrowing, eyes sharp.

Uh-oh, he thought, stifling a giggle. *Looks like there's a lecture on the way.*

Elizabeth cleared her throat. "You're not like other people, Ryan. You've got a serious problem."

"No, Elizabeth," Ryan began, struggling to hold back his laughter. "*You've* got a *serious* problem! Maybe you should attend some meetings to deal with it. 'Hi, my name is Elizabeth Wakefield,

164

and I'm serious.' Or better yet take a lesson or two from your sister. *She* knows how to enjoy herself."

"Ryan!" Elizabeth cried. "How can you twist my words like that? I'm trying to help you. You have a special problem—a *disease*. Alcohol could kill you. And you're acting like it's a joke!"

Ryan rolled his eyes. *It's time for Elizabeth to lighten up or leave,* he thought. "The only problem *I* have with drinking is when goody-goodies like you try to ruin my fun. *You* should try it sometime. If anyone needs to relax, it's you. Here." Ryan filled up the glass and shoved it in her face. "Go on," he urged. "This will cure your seriousness disease."

He watched as Elizabeth's face contorted, as if she was in pain. Her body heaved, and she burst into tears. "You were doing so well," she admonished him. "You'd been sober for so long . . . since before I met you. I was proud of you. And now look at you—you're a drunk. And an *obnoxious* one too. I can't believe you're ruining your life like this." She spun around and fled from his room, the door slamming behind her.

Oh, well, Ryan thought with a shrug. *I guess that means she won't be joining me. But that's OK, because I love to drink alone.* He raised the glass he'd poured for her to his lips and downed the whiskey in one neat swallow.

Chapter Ten

"Eight A.M.," Jessica murmured, catching sight of her clock radio. She flung back her soft blue bedspread. "Ugh! I was planning on sleeping till noon."

She sat up and swung her bare feet to the hardwood floor. *Oh, well,* she thought, smoothing down the front of her Chinese-style silk pajamas. *I can always take a catnap on the beach. It is my day off, after all. I should make the most of it.*

She stood up and gave her body a good stretch, reaching for the high ceiling. First one hand, then the other. She padded over to the large bay window and pushed aside the white lace curtains. "Oh!" she cried disappointedly. "Not fair!" The sky was a blanket of gray clouds. "Now what am I going to do?"

Jessica plopped down on her bed. She'd really wanted to work on her tan before hitting the clubs with Miranda, but the bad weather was threatening to mess up all her plans.

She switched on the radio to the SVU college station, hoping to hear something fast and furious to match her mood. But she found herself smiling when she recognized the haunting French voice that poured out instead. Edith Piaf. Ben had introduced Jessica to Piaf's music. She was one of Ben's favorites. *But I guess he's playing her records for Priya now,* she thought gloomily.

"Wait a minute," Jessica proclaimed, shaking off the dreary thought. "Isabella is in Paris with her boss this week! It's Wednesday afternoon there—maybe she'll be at the hotel."

She picked up the bedside phone and dialed the hotel number, hoping she'd be able to get through. Isabella Ricci, one of her best friends from SVU, had only just started her summer internship with a buyer in an exclusive New York City boutique and already she'd scored a free trip to Europe. Isabella had met Ben and Ryan on a quick visit the previous summer, but she wasn't personally involved in any of the goings-on at Sweet Valley Shore. She'd be the perfect person to help Jessica out of her romantic jam.

"Hotel Olivier. *Bonjour.*"

"*Bonjour.* Isabella Ricci, *s'il vous plaît?*" Jessica asked the receptionist, hoping her rusty French could be understood over the crackling connection. "*C'est* Jessica Wakefield."

After a brief pause Isabella's sweet laughter came tinkling over the line. *"Bonjour, Jessica, c'est moi!"*

"Izzy! Are you having a great time? Do you love Paris?"

"Oui. C'est magnifique!" Isabella laughed again. "Angelique and I viewed Patsy Dubonnet's collections today. Tomorrow we're off to Rome to see what Adolpho B. has planned for his winter resort line. Can you believe it?"

Jessica stifled a jealous groan. Why hadn't she had the sense to intern in the world of haute couture instead of resigning herself to a summer of waterlogged misery?

"What's going on with you?" Isabella continued. "Are you having a great time at the shore?"

Jessica hesitated. "Well, not exactly." She twirled the phone cord around one of her long, slender fingers.

"What is it?" Isabella asked. "I thought your summer was set. You had a job. You had a boyfriend—" Isabella's voice broke off, and Jessica could almost hear the wheels turning in her friend's head. "Uh-oh. What happened to Ben?"

Groaning, Jessica drew her knees to her chest. Isabella knew her too well. "He showed up with Priya," she mumbled.

"What? He showed up with a piranha?"

Jessica laughed in spite of her gloom. Isabella

always knew how to cheer her up, even if she wasn't half trying. "Not a piranha," she said with a giggle. "A girlfriend named Priya. But she is a man-eater, for sure."

Isabella chuckled. "You don't sound too broken up about it."

Jessica rolled onto her stomach and swung her pajama-clad legs up and down. "I guess I'm not. I mean, I'm still very interested in him. But—"

"There's another guy," Isabella cut in. Sometimes Jessica wondered why she even bothered speaking when she and Isabella talked. They seemed to have ESP, at least where men were concerned. "So why don't you go for him?"

Jessica's legs stopped swinging. "He's . . ." She lowered her voice and prayed no one in the house was listening. "He's Elizabeth's boyfriend, Ryan Taylor," she whispered. "You remember him—"

"Don't even think about it, Jessica," Isabella warned. "Don't do it to yourself."

Jessica sat up. "It's not like you think. Liz and Ryan aren't getting along at all."

"What are you going to do?"

Jessica sighed. "Nothing. I'm just going along as the dateless wonder. Before long I'll break my ninth-grade record—no dates in almost a month."

"That long!" Isabella laughed. "How did you possibly manage that?"

Jessica snorted. "Chicken pox. I was quarantined." Actually she'd only been quarantined for two days but had refused to go to school for a whole month until every single chicken pox spot on her face had completely disappeared. She giggled at the memory.

"Figures." Isabella laughed. "It was either that or you'd been marooned on a desert island."

Jessica shook her head. "It's not funny, Izzy. It feels like that's exactly what's happened here. I seem to be the only girl on Sweet Valley Shore who doesn't get noticed."

Suddenly a loud woman's voice could be heard in the background. "I'm really sorry, Jessica; I've got to go," Isabella called over it. "Angelique is here. There's a soiree beneath the Eiffel Tower tonight, and we have to get ready. But I'll call you from Rome as soon as I get there, OK? Au revoir."

"Au revoir," Jessica echoed. She hung up the phone, feeling slightly dejected. She'd joked with Isabella about her love life, but the truth was, it was no joke. It was a total disaster.

"No moping around," she told the empty room. "It's my day off." She changed out of her pajamas into the new French-cut, checkered bikini she'd "borrowed" the other day from Elizabeth's drawer. "With any luck the weather will change. And after a dip in the ocean and a long rest on the beach, it's going to seem like a whole new world."

She slipped on the matching black-and-white-checkered robe and headed downstairs. What she found made her feet stop in their tracks and her stomach threaten to revolt. Off to one side of the room, Ben and Priya were sorting through a laundry basket full of Ben's dirty clothes. Priya's lovely dark hair was twirled into a housewife's bun atop her head. The whole scene was nauseatingly domestic.

"How sweet," Jessica sneered. "I'm a bit surprised that intellectuals such as yourselves are willing to stoop to doing the everyday chores of us mere mortals."

Priya smiled sweetly, though Jessica could see the razor glint in her eyes. "Oh, I like tedious, practical subjects. What I don't like are tedious, practical people. There is a wide difference."

Jessica felt her face turn scarlet. "Tedious and practical!" she spat. "I'll have you know I'm one of the most *un*-practical people—"

Ben's loud laughter cut her off. He winked at Priya. "I know that one. Oscar Wilde. *An Ideal Husband*, right?"

Priya kissed him on the nose. "You brilliant man," she gushed. "Now as for Jessica's *im*-practicality—not *un*-practicality—I'd say . . ."

Jessica pretended to gag and then stomped toward the front door without bothering to hear the rest. The truth was, she didn't want Ben and

Priya to know how small they'd managed to make her feel—as if she barely even existed.

Elizabeth's sea green eyes scanned the choppy ocean water from Tower 2. Hardly anyone was out in the sea this morning. A few diehard surfers were clinging to their boards as the waves reared and churned, breaking dangerously close to the shore. The strong breeze was laced with a chill, and she wondered if they weren't in for a storm. She pulled her SVU sweatshirt on over her suit and nylon jacket for good measure.

"If Ryan were still head lifeguard," she murmured, "he would probably have us put the red warning flags out. Maybe even close the beach."

She rubbed her hands up and down on her arms and looked across the expanse of empty sand to where Nina was standing, binoculars poised, at Tower 4. *I could mention it to her, I guess,* Elizabeth thought, immediately dismissing it. "No," she muttered, shaking her head. "Nothing I say to Nina seems to come out right anymore. She would probably misunderstand, and we'd have another argument. I guess I could try Ryan. Then he could tell Nina."

Elizabeth's eyes turned to the main tower. Her thoughts had been drifting there all morning in one way or another. "Poor Ryan," she whispered. "I've got to do something. He desperately needs my help."

If only I'd met him for his sobriety celebration, she thought, chewing guiltily on her lip. *He wouldn't have taken that first drink.*

She looked back at the frothing surf. The last two surfers had given up and come in. "Miranda can cover for me," Elizabeth reasoned. "I'm no good here if all I think about is Ryan anyway."

Elizabeth climbed down from her post and headed to Miranda's. As she walked through the cool sand she felt suddenly lighter. "It's time for some tough love," she resolved. "Ryan needs a strong hand to guide him back to sobriety. I'm his girlfriend. I'm the one who needs to do it."

"Hey, Liz," Miranda called, waving from Tower 3. "What's going on with this weather? I'm freezing."

Elizabeth looked up. "I don't know, but it's sure keeping the tourists away. Did you forget your foul weather clothes?"

Miranda grinned. "I met this really cute guy jogging on the boardwalk last night. He said he might come to the beach today, and I didn't want him to see me in my baggy sweats. So instead I look like a plucked chicken, complete with goose bumps. Remind me not to be so silly, will you?"

Elizabeth smiled and held on to her long blond ponytail to keep it from whipping across her face. "Sure thing. And I have a warm proposition for you."

Miranda sat forward, her strong shoulders rigid and tense from the chill. "Shoot."

"Would you cover for me for a little while? I have sweatpants and an extra sweater at my chair."

Miranda leaped up and jumped down onto the sand. "For warm clothes I'll do anything!"

"Thanks, Miranda. I'll try not to be too long." She started toward the main tower. When she reached Ryan's living quarters, she softly called, "Ryan?" and knocked lightly. There was no answer, so she tried the knob. The door swung open, revealing the darkened room.

"Phew," Elizabeth whispered, holding her nose. A sickly sweet mixture of sweat and alcohol hit her like a tidal wave. She fumbled her way along the wall until she reached the windowsill. Then she pulled up the blinds and flung open the window, taking a deep breath of fresh air before turning to see what the morning light had revealed.

Ryan was lying facedown and motionless across the bed, one foot touching the floor. His hand trailed down off the bed, just inches from the overturned whiskey bottle she'd seen him with the previous night. He was still dressed in his jeans and stained polo shirt; his clothes were a disheveled mess. He'd only managed to remove one sneaker.

"Ryan!" Elizabeth cried, shaking him. "Wake up."

Ryan groaned, raising his head slightly before letting it sink back onto his pillow.

"Come on, Ryan."

He swatted at her but missed, knocking over his lamp instead.

Elizabeth scurried around him and righted it with a slam. *"Now!"* she demanded.

Ryan turned over onto his back and pushed himself up by his arms. He opened one swollen eye. "Not you," he said with a groan. "I thought I got rid of you last night." He reached down for the overturned bottle of whiskey.

Elizabeth grabbed the bottle. "You'll have to be quicker than that," she countered. She held the bottle up to the light of the window. There were a few drops left. "It's all about hand-eye coordination, Ryan, remember? Now watch!" She reared back and heaved the bottle out the open window. She would pick it up off the beach and throw it away when she left.

"Hey!" Ryan complained, stumbling to his feet. "That was perfectly good whiskey. Why'd you do that?"

Elizabeth turned on him, her eyes blazing. "Because you've had enough," she shouted. "Pull your life back together."

Ryan sucked in his breath and fell back onto his bed, one arm thrown across his forehead. "Shhh. Your voice hurts my brain."

Elizabeth loomed over him, staring down at the wreck of the man she'd once felt so much for. "Ryan, please," she begged. "Can't you see how self-destructive you're being?"

He blinked once and narrowed his bloodshot eyes. "It's only self-destructive in your mind. This is what I am. And if you can't relax and love me—drinking and all—then get lost."

Elizabeth froze, a mottled flush spreading up from her neck. All she'd been trying to do was help Ryan, but he was throwing her love back in her face. She squared her shoulders and glared at him. "Why not?" she spat. "You're *already* lost!" She dashed out of the room before he could see her angry tears.

"C'mon, sunshine!" Nina coaxed, still twisting her hands anxiously, her dark eyes sweeping up and down the shoreline.

The threat of an early morning tempest was slowly but surely being replaced by a late morning calm. The temperature had risen a good five degrees in the past fifteen minutes as the forbidding clouds that had been hanging over the beach were being blown out to sea. *Thank goodness,* she thought.

The water was still a bit rough, but the sun was shining and Nina could easily see that the ocean was going to be manageable. Beachgoers who had been huddling under their sweatshirts and jeans were quickly peeling them off to reveal their bathing suits. From the boardwalk the usual hordes of sunseekers were streaming onto the beach. It was turning into business as usual.

"No need to close the beach now," Nina told herself. But what about earlier? Had she taken too big of a chance? She couldn't help wondering whether she'd done the right thing in keeping the beach open.

Nina rubbed her eyes and leaned forward in her lifeguard chair. "I'm not up to this," she muttered. "Ryan would have known what to do intuitively, but I need to hear what other people think first."

Despite the warming sun Nina felt a chill pass through her body. "What other people?" she whispered. "I've broken up with two boyfriends in one week and alienated my best friend on top of it."

Nina pulled off her own hooded sweatshirt and dragged her mind back to her lifeguard duties. A group of kids had headed out into the water and were clinging to a rubber dinghy. Now they were drifting out into the deeper water. Nina stood and blew her whistle, waving her arm for them to move closer to shore.

Just like my life, she thought as she sat down again. *I'm in deep water here. I'm in love with a guy I'm not sure I can trust. I've got a job I might not be able to handle. I have a best friend I'm barely speaking to.*

"I'm being swept out by the undertow," she whispered, leaning her elbows on the wooden railing. "How do I keep from drowning?"

The memory of Stu's handsome, sweet-tempered face appeared before her. Stu could keep her from drowning. He could relieve her loneliness—if only she would let him.

"But how can I?" she complained, resting her chin in her hands. "As good as he's been to me, can I really trust him?"

Nina stared out at the surging ocean, her lips trembling. The thought of Stu with another woman made her sick, but the thought of life without Stu was even worse.

She brushed a tear from the corner of her eye. "I'll be fine," she insisted. "It's my own fault anyway. If I'd kept my vow of no men for the summer, I wouldn't be in this pain. I should have listened to myself."

She glanced down at the fine white sand, now sprinkled with sunbathers lying on towels and setting up beach umbrellas. Nearly everyone seemed to be part of a group or a couple, either among friends or with a partner. "From now on I'll be alone," Nina murmured sadly, her eyes drifting down the beach. "Just like that woman."

Nina let her eyes linger on the young

woman's peculiar appearance. Pretty much all the beachgoers were in bathing suits, shorts, and T-shirts, but the blond woman had most of her body concealed by a billowing housecoat.

"Weird," Nina commented, staring at the big, round sunglasses that hid the woman's face.

But with a start Nina realized it wasn't just the young woman's costume that set off alarms in her mind. It was the fact that she was sitting with her back to the ocean, staring straight at Nina.

"But this guy's supposed to be the best," Winston insisted as he paced around the Paloma beach house pool. "He's the healer to the stars. Even an unnamed ex-president's wife goes to him!"

Wendy made a face as she slathered a big gob of suntan lotion on her legs. "Not interested."

"But . . . but . . . ," Winston stuttered. "I practically had to bribe his assistant to fit us in. He has princesses and duchesses flying in from all over the world to consult with him. The least you could do is meet with the guy."

"No, Winston," Wendy protested, her face set in a determined pout. "I've done enough soul-searching. Pedro and I are through." She adjusted the strap of her blue-and-green-gingham bikini before burying her nose in her Agatha Christie mystery. "Fortunately it's turned into a beautiful day, and I intend to enjoy it for all it's worth."

Enjoy? Ha! Winston argued silently as he studied the rigid set of her jaw. It seemed impossible for Wendy to enjoy anything lately. Even with dark designer sunglasses covering her eyes, Winston could tell she'd spent another night crying. *I'm not giving up on you yet, Wendy. I'm a bulldog of determination.*

Wendy shifted her position slightly as she reclined on the chaise longue. "Will you please stop staring at me?" she said in exasperation. "I've read the same paragraph three times, and I still don't know what the murder weapon was."

Winston sighed and shoved his hands into the pockets of his khaki shorts. "Wendy, I heard you crying last night. If you're so sure you don't care about Pedro anymore, then why are you still upset?"

Groaning, Wendy threw the book aside. "I'm not. I'd been watching a sad movie, that's all."

Winston dropped down on the patio chair next to her. He'd been watching the same movie in his room, and it was a comedy. "You don't make a very good liar. Why don't you at least call Pedro? He doesn't even know you feel this way."

Wendy shook her head and hugged her knees. "What's the use? I know what he's going to say. 'I love you, Wendy, but I've got to finish this tour.' And then there'll be the next one and the one after that."

Winston ran a hand through his brown curls. "You've got to tell him sometime. Or are you thinking of packing up and leaving before he gets back?"

180

Wendy grimaced and began to trace the outline of her bare toes with her finger. "I'll wait until he gets here," she mumbled. "But then I'm packing."

Winston consulted the date on his watch. "That gives us at least a week. So come on, what can it hurt to talk to a psychic healer? We might even bump into some stars."

Wendy groaned and dropped her chin on her knees. "What's the point? I don't love Pedro anymore, and no guru-swami stargazer is going to change that."

"He's a crystal reader."

Wendy waved her slender hand in a dismissive gesture. "Whatever. I still don't see how it's of any relevance to me."

Winston crossed his arms and tipped back his chair. *If Wendy didn't love Pedro anymore, she'd have a point,* he thought. *But she does love him. I'm sure of it.* And he was sure if he could get Wendy to talk to the psychic, she'd know it too.

"We're not *doing* anything here," he said innocently. "Why don't we go for a ride?" He'd already made the appointment for eleven that morning; the man's assistant had warned him not to be late. "You promised me I could take your big blue Mercedes for a spin."

"I'm working on my tan."

"Come on, Wendy, it's not good to get too much sun."

181

Wendy looked at him and smirked. "Then I guess that makes you the healthiest person at Sweet Valley Shore."

Winston looked down at his pale, knobby knees and gulped. "For that you get splashed!" he threatened. He jumped up, dashed to the side of the pool, and splashed a handful of cold water on Wendy.

"OK, OK!" she screamed, trying to block the water with her hands. "I'll let you take me for a drive."

Winston smiled and sat up on his haunches. "I'll even buy you lunch."

Wendy made a face as she stood up and quickly pulled a stretchy green summer dress over her head. "Lunch? You don't have a job, remember? Where are you going to get money for lunch?"

Winston stood up and dried his hands on her beach towel. "I still have some clout left over from last summer. I have carte blanche at Hamburger Harry's, remember?"

Wendy wrinkled her nose as she slipped on her leather sandals. "All right, I'll have lunch with you, but under one condition."

Winston cocked his head. "What's that?"

"*I* pick where we go, and *I* pay. After last summer I never want to eat at Hamburger Harry's again."

Chapter Eleven

Your days are numbered, the young woman thought gleefully as she stared up at Nina. A wicked smile played across her lips. *And I'm the one ticking them off.*

She shifted on her striped beach towel, stretching her long, slender legs so her bare heels touched the warm sand. "The first thing I'll do when I move into Stuart's beach house is burn all of these rags," she muttered, looking down at her drab, flowered housecoat with disgust. "With his money he can afford to buy me a brand-new wardrobe."

She ran a hand through her short blond hair and grimaced. She'd be growing that back as well. "Soon I'll be Mrs. Stuart Kirkwood." It had the perfect ring—as in *wedding* ring. "After last night it's in the bag."

The young woman leaned back on her elbows and replayed the scene she'd witnessed the previous night. She'd chosen her usual hideout in the tall reeds near Stu's beach house, where she could see everything without being discovered. The memory of Nina's face, in all its heartbreak and confusion, floated back to her. "Run along now," she whispered as she recalled how Nina had fled Stu's house in tears.

The young woman licked her lips. "Another brilliant idea," she muttered, hugging herself with pride. "Sending Stuart that love letter was a stroke of genius." But then, foolishly and without meaning to, she let the memory continue.

The young woman felt her throat catch, and she swallowed hard. Suddenly she was back in the tall reeds near Stu's house, the elation at Nina's flight still causing her chest to swell. But what happened next had made her smile shrivel and her beating heart freeze. The slow-motion replay continued: Stu crushing the letter in his fist and throwing it into the fire. Stu sinking to his knees and calling Nina's name.

"No!" she cried out, drawing strange glances from the people lounging on beach towels around her.

The young woman winced and dug her hands angrily into the warm sand. "He's confused," she whispered to herself vehemently.

"As soon as he sees me, we'll be in each other's arms again."

She turned her gaze furiously toward Nina. "It won't be long now," she threatened under her breath. "I'll be ready to show myself and take my rightful place beside Stuart. And you will be discarded like an old, drab newspaper."

The young woman brushed off the sand from her hands and then rubbed her belly through the dingy housecoat. "Nobody can deny the power of fate," she said with a smirk. "But sometimes it needs a little nudge to set it in motion. To make sure the right people stay together forever . . ." She looked back at Nina. "Poor thing," she hissed. "You don't have a clue, do you?"

I could let you go, she told Nina silently, *but what fun would that be? If prison has taught me anything, it's that anyone who sticks their nose where it doesn't belong gets punished. Severely.*

"Winston, pull over," Wendy complained. "We're totally lost."

Winston hid a smile and played footsie with the gas pedal. "I can't. It must be the, you know, *nobelium.* If the modulator is off, the car will stall. We'll never get it started again."

Wendy snorted. "Don't try to pull a fast one on me, Winston Egbert. I had three brothers, remember? I know there's no such thing as a nobelium or a modulator in a car."

Winston gulped and hit the gas hard. They were almost at the crystal healer's house. A few more tricky maneuvers and they'd be in time for Wendy's appointment.

"Winston!" Wendy yelled. "Slow down!" She poked her head out the car window. "Didn't that sign say Sweet Valley Shore to the right?"

Winston shrugged and made a hard left, racing up into the craggy terrain of the desert hills.

Wendy gripped the dashboard. "What are you doing?" she screeched. "We're in no-man's-land here. All I can see is desert sand and cacti! You've got to turn around."

Winston grimaced, concentrating hard on the dusty dirt road. The crystal reader's assistant had told him two lefts and then a turn at a yellow mailbox. He'd done the two lefts, but where was that mailbox? Where was anything?

Wendy's right, he thought with a groan. *We are in no-man's-land. Next we're going to be surrounded by a pack of wild coyotes!*

"Sorry, Wendy," he stalled. "The wheel seems to be out of control. It must be the lufwhacker!"

Suddenly the yellow mailbox came into view. Winston cut the wheel to the left and bumped them over a line of tumbleweeds. They lurched to a stop outside a large pink house.

"Thank goodness," Wendy cried, rubbing the dust from her eyes. "Let's hope they have a phone or at least can point us in the right direction. We've got to get out of here." She stepped out of the car.

Winston covertly glanced at his watch. Ten fifty-nine A.M. "Perfect timing," he murmured, grinning.

Wendy stuck her head through the open window. "What was that?"

Winston gave her his most innocent smile. "Nothing. Let's go say hi to our saviors."

The woman who opened the door gave them a matter-of-fact nod and motioned them to follow her down a long hallway carpeted in thick red pile with black geometric shapes. She quickly concealed her hands in the sleeves of her long kimono.

"Winston," Wendy whispered, clutching his arm through his yellow fifties-style bowling shirt. "Tell her we need to use the phone." She was pulling at the skirt of her lime green dress anxiously.

Winston gulped. If he hadn't been the one who'd arranged this meeting, he'd be spooked too. He grimaced as they passed a bookcase containing a row of polished human skulls. *Come to think of it,* he thought, *I'm spooked anyway!*

The woman turned to them, her luminous dark eyes seeming to grow larger by the second. "Please, the Master does not like to be kept waiting."

Winston felt Wendy's grip on his arm get even tighter. "Master?" she gasped under her breath. "Excuse me, but all we need are directions."

The woman nodded. "Of course. That is why you are here to see the Master."

"See, Wendy, we're in good hands here," Winston murmured as he nervously followed the receptionist. He gulped when the next display case caught his eye; it was filled with plaster casts of outstretched human hands. *Bad choice of words,* he thought.

The woman pushed open a massive, creaking door that opened into an enormous room bathed in golden light. "Enter," a deep, booming voice called out.

Winston swallowed audibly and pulled Wendy in with him. The man with the thunderous voice was sitting cross-legged in front of a low table covered with a black velvet cloth. He was dressed from head to toe in black, and his white hair seemed to stick out in all directions.

"You must be Wendy." His baritone voice rang out in the sparsely furnished room. He held out his arm, hand twisted sideways. "I am Master Chalmers. But you can refer to me as William."

Wendy seemed paralyzed, her mouth gaping open. Winston gave her a discreet push. "Say hello, Wendy."

"Hello, Wendy," she squeaked, tumbling forward.

Master Chalmers's thin lips curled into a smile. He pointed to a large square pillow on the floor opposite him. "You may take that seat."

Winston herded her over and pressed down on her shoulders, causing her to sit. Wendy looked up at him, her eyes frightened until suddenly, angrily, realization dawned on her. "Winston Egbert," she spat, "this was a setup!" She turned to Master Chalmers. "You're the crystal reader, aren't you?"

Master Chalmers nodded and reached behind him. He pulled out a purple velvet bag and removed a set of translucent crystals. "Please arrange these in a pattern that pleases you."

Wendy scrunched up her face. "And if I don't?"

Master Chalmers frowned. "Then I can be of no service to you. You do want answers, don't you?"

"Yes." Winston nodded vigorously and turned to Wendy. "We're here. You might as well give it a try."

Wendy narrowed her eyes and reluctantly picked up the first crystal. It was a transparent, teardrop-shaped piece of quartz that twinkled when the light caught it, reflecting a rainbow of colors on the low, velvet-covered table. Immediately a sense of peace came over Wendy's face, softening it.

When she was done arranging the crystals, Master Chalmers let out a deep breath, rolled his lean shoulders, and cleared his throat. "The pattern suggests that your true love is away on a long trip." He cocked his head, massaging the ridge of his nose between his eyes. "There is a distance between you." He picked up one of the crystals and looked up at Wendy. "Do you see how it is shaped like a boat?"

Wendy shrugged, and Winston could see she wasn't buying any of it—not yet.

Master Chalmers nodded and placed the crystal back. "It is causing you a great deal of pain," he said softly.

Wendy winced but remained silent.

Master Chalmers sucked in a deep breath and picked up one of the crystals Wendy had placed far from the others. "This shows there is uncertainty. Maybe even a bold move."

Winston nodded. *That's for sure,* he thought. *Leaving Pedro is about as bold a move as Wendy could make.*

Master Chalmers bent his head. "Hmmm . . . very interesting."

"What?" Winston broke in.

"From what the rest of the pattern shows, Wendy and this faraway person are meant for each other."

"See, Wendy?" Winston cheered. "It's as clear as

190

a bell. You and Pedro are meant to be together!"

Wendy narrowed her eyes. "Who said anything about Pedro? There's lots of people I know who are far away. It's summer vacation, remember?"

Winston groaned and turned to the crystal reader. "Do you see anything else?"

Master Chalmers picked up one last crystal. "This one has been placed in such a way that its shape looks like a guitar. Could this true love's profession have something to do with music?"

Winston crossed his arms and nodded at Wendy, only half suppressing a gloating I-told-you-so smile.

Wendy closed her open mouth and quickly wiped the astonishment from her face. "Could have been a lucky guess," she muttered.

Suddenly Master Chalmers gave a slight groan, putting his hands to his head.

"Are you all right?" Winston asked.

The old man nodded. "It is difficult work," he told them.

The receptionist suddenly entered the room and gave two loud claps. "Master Chalmers must rest now," she announced sternly.

Winston helped Wendy to her feet and followed the receptionist as they retraced their steps through the house. After Wendy paid for the reading, the woman nodded to them curtly and closed the door behind them. That was it. The visit was over.

Silently they headed back to Wendy's blue Mercedes. "You see," Winston began as he turned the key in the ignition, "you and Pedro are definitely meant to be together. All the signs point to it."

Wendy crossed her arms. "Maybe it's OK for you, Winston. But I'm not basing my life on advice from fire walkers, chakra gurus, or master crystal readers. I know Pedro and I are through, no matter what the crackpots of this world have to say."

"Shouldn't you be at work?" Elizabeth asked, slightly annoyed. She and Jessica were by the beach house. At her feet Jessica was lying on a large sheet surrounded by suntan products, several glossy fashion magazines, a spritzer bottle full of water, and a large red cooler.

Jessica pulled on the fabric of her bikini bottom to check her tan line. "Jealous? It's my day off. Fortunately it turned out to be a gorgeous day. I was worried when I woke up."

Elizabeth glowered as she removed her sunglasses, letting them dangle around her neck on their cloth safety cord. "That checkered bikini looks awfully familiar, Jess. Isn't it *mine?*"

Jessica lowered her long eyelashes in a show of innocence. "Is it? It's hard to tell since we wear the same size. I get confused sometimes."

"But you would have remembered buying it! I hadn't even removed the price tags yet."

Jessica laughed. "Sorry, Liz, but all my suits were sandy."

"You could have washed one out."

"But I *hate* putting on a swimsuit when it's all wet. Eeew, it's the grossest feeling."

Elizabeth rolled her eyes. "Swimsuits are *meant* to get wet, Jessica."

"Jeez, I'm sorry," Jessica added, honestly looking repentant. "Were you saving this one to surprise Ryan?"

Suddenly Elizabeth's anger went into overdrive. "Not anymore," she spat. "I'm done with Ryan. We're over."

Jessica sat up, her blue-green eyes widening. "What happened?"

Elizabeth scowled and dropped down onto the sand next to her sister. "He's—" She stopped short. Was it right to tell Jessica about Ryan's drinking? Ryan had always been supersecret about his sobriety. Why should she break his confidentiality now?

"He's acting like a total stranger," Elizabeth amended. "When I ask why, he pushes me away. That's all." She pulled the band from her ponytail and shook out her hair. "But it doesn't matter now. I don't care anymore. I'm washing my hands of the whole situation."

"Are you sure?" Jessica asked. "Isn't there a lot between you two that still hasn't been resolved?"

Elizabeth made a face. *How can I resolve anything when Ryan won't even talk to me?* she wondered. *Now that he's drinking, he's totally incommunicado.* "Nothing I care to work on," she stated flatly. "From now on Ryan can do whatever he wants. I'm out of it."

Jessica brushed some sand from the sheet. "But you two were so happy."

"Were," Elizabeth cut in, feeling her mood begin to darken even more. She looked away from her sister, focusing on the rhythmic beat of the waves. She was soothed for a moment; then, as if she were trying to sabotage her own temporary peace of mind, her gaze fell on the corner of the main tower where Ryan's room was situated. Her stomach twisted, and she forced herself to close her eyes. "We're not happy now," she muttered.

"But don't you still have feelings for him?"

Elizabeth turned and stared hard at her sister. "What is this? I thought you'd be on my side. Are you trying to keep Ryan and me together?"

Jessica shrugged. "I'm trying to make sure you know what you're doing." She reached for her suntan lotion. "I'd hate for you to say all this and not really mean it."

Elizabeth wrapped her arms around her body and hugged herself tightly as the vision of the belligerent, hungover Ryan from this morning came back to her. *Whoever that person is,* she thought, *there's not a trace of the Ryan I used to love in him.*

Elizabeth shook her head to clear it. "Don't worry about that. I've never been more sure about anything. It's completely over between us."

Jessica cocked her head as she rubbed the suntan lotion liberally up and down her legs. "I guess you know what you're saying, then."

Elizabeth nodded adamantly. "I don't feel anything for Ryan anymore. In fact, I just feel numb—like I never felt anything for him in the first place. Do you know what I mean?"

"Yes." Jessica snorted. "I think I can safely say Ben fits into that category."

Elizabeth rocked back on her heels. "Exactly. We Wakefields can take only so much abuse, and then that's it." She stood up and slipped on her sunglasses, trying to ignore the clenching of her heart. "I've reached my limit. I'm glad Ryan's quitting the squad, even if Nina doesn't want the job. Because the sooner our ties are severed, the better."

"Well, at least you didn't deceive me about lunch," Wendy mumbled, forlornly pushing a piece of romaine around her salad plate with her fork.

Winston sighed when he caught a glimpse of his friend's unhappy face. Even though they were in one of the fanciest cafés in Sweet Valley Shore, Wendy hardly seemed to notice.

"I don't understand why you're feeling down,"

Winston began, gesturing around the room. Everywhere he looked was another special touch— from the abundant flower arrangements to the three-piece combo playing mellow jazz in the background. "This place is amazing."

"It's not the restaurant. It's what happened earlier."

Winston scowled and poured them both more sparkling water. "But I would think that what Master Chalmers said would be good news."

Wendy let her fork clatter to her plate and hung her head, letting her dark hair obscure her face. "Where did you come up with that idea?"

"Come on, don't be sad," Winston pleaded, reaching over to massage Wendy's bare arm. "Everything is looking up. All our attempts at getting to the bottom of your feelings are pointing universally to how much you love Pedro. You should be celebrating."

Wendy pushed her plate away and buried her face in her hands. "Maybe I loved him once," she blurted. "But it's not true now." To Winston's horror, she burst into tears.

"Wendy!" Winston gasped. He was up in a flash, scooting around the table to kneel by her side. He wrapped his arm around her heaving shoulders. "What is it? Why are you crying?"

She shook her head, holding up her hand for him to back away. Winston reluctantly returned to his seat, his heart saddened. He hated to see her in distress.

"It was all the soul-searching, wasn't it?" he said anxiously. "I'm sorry. I should never have pushed you that hard. You would have seen how much you still loved Pedro sooner or later."

Wendy remained silent, her thin shoulders shuddering under the weight of her sobs.

Winston twisted the linen tablecloth and fretted. He'd never felt so helpless before. "Wendy, please," he begged, "talk to me."

Finally Wendy pulled her hands away from her face. Her tears still streamed down her cheeks, but she seemed calmer. "I've got something to tell you," she whimpered, her chin trembling.

"What?" Winston asked softly, taking his napkin and dabbing at her eyes.

"It's about me and Pedro . . . and . . ."

"Yes?" Winston prompted. "And the fact that you've realized how much you love him?"

Wendy shook her head and grabbed Winston's hand. "No, not Pedro. You."

Winston cocked his head. "Me? What are you talking about?"

"It's you, Winston," Wendy gushed. "Not Pedro. I've finally realized how much I love *you*."

Chapter Twelve

"So you wouldn't even care if Ryan dated someone *else*?"

Jessica moistened her lips and waited for Elizabeth to answer. *This is the ultimate test,* she thought. *If Liz says she doesn't care about that, then she must be serious about her and Ryan being through.*

Elizabeth shook her head vehemently. "I wouldn't care if he paraded around Sweet Valley Shore with a girl on each arm. I'm through with him."

Jessica raised one eyebrow nonchalantly and picked up the spritzer bottle from her sheet. She gave her lean, tanned body a few squirts of cold water to cool it off. "You wouldn't be even a little jealous?"

"Nope. If someone else wants to deal with him, that's her problem." Elizabeth brushed her hands and placed them on her hips with a flourish.

Jessica sat up on her knees. "Good for you, Liz.

I'm proud of you. I mean, if Ryan's acting like a jerk around you, then who needs him, right?"

Elizabeth grinned and bent down, giving Jessica a big hug. "Thanks for the support," she murmured. "I knew you'd understand."

Jessica flicked back her hair. "Of course. Why stay with Ryan if it's not working out? There's nothing worse than feeling unwanted."

That's the understatement of the year, Jessica thought, her mind flashing on all the horrible things Ben and Priya had done to make her feel like an invisible woman and a total failure.

"Exactly." Elizabeth nodded her blond head resolutely. "Well, I'd better get back to my post. I left poor Miranda covering the fort. She's going to be wondering what happened to me."

Jessica giggled. "Just don't wear her out. She and I are planning to hit the clubs tonight. Anyway, don't worry. She's happy as long as she's out of the way of that horrible Priya."

"OK." Elizabeth grinned. "And thanks for the pep talk, Jess. I know I'm doing the right thing . . . but it's always nice to hear you say so too."

"Anytime." Jessica laughed, waving as Elizabeth walked away. Jessica lay back down on her towel, a Cheshire cat's grin creeping across her face. Elizabeth had practically given Jessica the go-ahead to move in on Ryan. It seemed too good to be true!

But does she mean it? Jessica wondered. *Sometimes people say one thing when they mean another.* Jessica had certainly blown hot and cold on plenty of men in the past.

"Maybe I'd better wait and see what happens," she murmured. "When Liz says she doesn't care who dates Ryan, she's probably not including me." It was one thing to see a stranger on your ex-boyfriend's arm; it was another to see your own twin sister.

Jessica turned onto her stomach, feeling the heat of the sand warming her through the sheet. But she just couldn't get Ryan's rugged good looks out of her mind.

She reached for the bottle of mineral water in her cooler. "Well, nothing says I can't pay Ryan a little social call before I go out tonight," she reasoned, unscrewing the plastic bottle cap. "*Someone* should look in on him and make sure he's taking all of this OK."

After all, Ryan is *my friend,* she thought, gulping her water and wiping her mouth. *He's never made* me *feel unwanted or invisible. In fact, he's made me feel anything but.*

Winston jerked his hand away as if he'd burned it on a hot stove, sending his water glass flying across the table. "You love *me?*" he gasped. "What do you mean?"

Wendy sat forward in her chair and righted the glass. "I mean—"

At that moment a waiter rushed up, interrupting them. "Is everything all right, sir?"

Winston shuddered and waved him away. *Everything is fine,* he thought. *Except that the whole world has just turned on its head!* Wendy dabbed at the spilled water with her napkin. "You've always been there for me," she murmured. "You've given me so much support these last few days—"

"As a *friend,*" Winston cut in. "I've done what any friend would do."

"No. You've done more than that. You helped me to get in touch with my feelings. You care about me."

Winston gnawed on his lower lip. "Maybe I've done more for you than I would have for most people, but that's because I really like you." Immediately he winced and bit his tongue, hoping his friendly words wouldn't be taken the wrong way. But his stomach lurched when he saw Wendy burst into a glowing smile.

Idiot! Winston chastised himself. *"I really like you." What a stupid thing to say. But that's not the same thing as love . . . is it?* He took a deep breath. *No. I have Denise Waters, who means more to me than anything. And Wendy is a married woman. I like her as a friend. Just a friend.*

Wendy beckoned him with her large gray

eyes. "Winston, we belong together. I know it."

"But . . . b-but . . . ," Winston stuttered. "But you belong with Pedro. He's your dream come true. I introduced you two."

"I was blind." Wendy reached over to touch his face, sending dangerous shock waves through his spine. "I should have seen then how much you cared for me. You knew I had a crush on Pedro, so you arranged that first date. But instead of pursuing my silly little fantasy, I should have stopped and looked at the person who made it possible. I should have married you, not Pedro."

Winston gulped so loudly, he was sure the whole restaurant heard it. The collar of his bowling shirt suddenly seemed to shrink by three sizes. "Ummm . . . let's not do anything drastic yet."

"How can we help ourselves?" Wendy purred, gazing at him longingly.

Suddenly it hit him—a genius plan that would fix everything. "Uh, Wendy, I need you to visit one more person," he said urgently. "A top-notch guru. Just one more, please?"

"No, Winston," she said firmly. "We've been through all that. I know it's you I love. I don't need anyone else telling me how I feel."

The back of Winston's neck tingled feverishly. He knew what he had to say next. Even though it felt horribly wrong, it was his only chance. "Wendy, if . . . if you really love me, then do this for me."

Wendy sighed and leaned her chin in her hands. "OK. For you, I'll go to one last guru. But then we should discuss our living arrangements. There's no reason for you to be sleeping all the way down the hall anymore, Winston."

Winston pulled on his collar. *If this plan doesn't cut it,* he realized with trepidation, *then we're* all *in big trouble.*

Jessica hummed to herself as she applied the finishing touches to her makeup. She leaned forward on the pink-cushioned stool before her vanity table and widened her eyes. "Hmmm . . . how about Midnight Blue?"

The new eyeliner glided onto the rim of her bottom lids like a dream. Pleased, she picked up a shimmering taupe eye shadow and brushed it over her upper lids.

"Almost there," she said admiringly. Then, with a subtle touch of Raspberry Razzle on her lips, her face was complete. "Perfect," she pronounced, examining the overall effect in the vanity table's mirror. "Now, what to wear?"

Jessica walked over to her closet and began flipping through her outfits. Since few of her clothes were actually hanging there, she began sifting through the things she'd left strewn about the room. Even though she'd arrived days ago, she hadn't really taken the time to unpack yet.

"Ho-hum," she complained. "I've already worn all the good stuff. Maybe that's why I can't turn any heads around here."

Except one, she amended, her smile widening as her mind involuntarily wandered to the memory of Ryan's gorgeous face and toned, tanned torso. *A head on the body of a bronze god.*

"Stop it, Jess!" she reprimanded herself. "When you drop by Ryan's tonight, it's strictly a mercy call. He's probably still heartsick about Liz. You're getting dressed up for the *available* guys out there."

But Ryan is *available,* a teasing voice reminded her.

Jessica gritted her teeth, pushing away the thought and turning back to rummaging through her clothes. "No one is going to notice me in any of this stuff," she muttered as she trudged over to her bed.

What am I going to do? she fumed. *I don't have time to shop. And with Liz hitting me up for half the money to repair the Jeep, I can't afford it anyway.* She threw herself backward onto her bed, hugging one of the throw pillows to her chest.

Wait a minute! she thought, sitting up with a jolt. *Since I'm paying for half the Jeep, Liz owes me.* A mischievous smile spread across her face.

"Isn't that what having a twin sister is all about? Sharing clothes?" she asked herself. She would go shopping where she could afford it—The House of Elizabeth!

Jessica slipped into her sister's room and closed the door silently behind her. She rifled quickly through Elizabeth's closet, not even trying on most of the clothes she found.

"No wonder Ryan's gotten tired of her," Jessica quipped, wrinkling her nose as she held up a plain blue dress. "These are clothes only a Girl Scout would love." She tossed the dress aside and reached for another. "I was having better luck in my own closet."

Jessica was about to give up when she came upon a sheer white blouse and a long, white, raw-silk skirt hiding in the farthest reaches of Elizabeth's closet.

"Hmmm . . . I wonder what Liz was saving these for." She held the pieces against her and studied her image in the full-length mirror.

The cut of the clothes didn't exactly get the Jessica Wakefield seal of approval. She would have preferred something a little more formfitting and short. But the white looked great with her tan, and the blouse was sheer—a little too sheer, to be exact. She'd get attention in it, all right, most likely in the form of a ticket for indecent exposure. But what else was there?

"Genius!" Jessica cried as she ran over to where Elizabeth kept her swimsuits. She knew her sister had a shimmering white maillot hidden away somewhere. It would make the perfect bodysuit.

"Here it is! Perfect!" Jessica wriggled out of her clothes and put on the swimsuit, then the silk skirt. They were a perfect match. The sheer shirt went on next; the sleeves were billowy and the tail was a little long, so Jessica tied it at her waist. From Elizabeth's line of carefully arranged shoes, Jessica picked her good white sandals. Her quest over, she admired herself in the mirror. "No one can put together an outfit like me," she boasted proudly, overjoyed with the results.

A few minutes later, after checking her hair and putting on one last dab of lipstick, Jessica headed downstairs. She rolled her eyes as the sound of Priya's voice came drifting up to her from the kitchen. "Doesn't that girl have her own home?" Jessica snarled. The last thing she wanted now was a run-in with Priya. With any luck she could slip out of the beach house without being seen.

She tiptoed down the stairs and was halfway to the door when Ben's voice rang out. "My, my, my," he said with a laugh, jumping up from the living-room sofa in his red swim trunks. "Don't we look nice. Priya," he called. "Come and take a look at this."

Jessica flashed her eyes at him. "Get out of my way, Ben," she fumed.

Priya came running in, wearing a faded T-shirt over her lifeguard suit. As soon as her eyes met Jessica's her brows shot up. "Gorgeous," she sneered. "But let me give you a word of advice. When a man's not interested in you, all the glamour in the world won't turn his head." She walked over to Ben and wrapped her arms around him, giving him a soft kiss on the cheek.

Jessica glowered. "Don't worry, Priya, this isn't for *your* boyfriend. Or anyone else's, for that matter. Tonight I'm going out and dancing till dawn. So if it's not too much trouble, would you please get out of my way? I'm finding you homebodies a big bore."

Jessica watched with satisfaction as Ben and Priya's mouths dropped open. "Toodles," she said with a giggle, winking as she skipped past them toward the main tower for her first stop of the evening.

Ryan lifted the sticky glass and made a toast. "To good riddance," he mumbled, bringing the glass to his lips and knocking back the burning dregs of whiskey. He licked his lips to be sure he caught every drop.

He'd lost count of the number of toasts he'd made about an hour ago, though the subject was still clear in his mind. The subject was the successful expulsion of that do-gooder Elizabeth Wakefield from his life.

You've been drinking all afternoon on an empty stomach, champ, a voice in his head cautioned him. *Why don't you eat something and sober up a little?*

Ryan focused his unsteady eyes on the passageway leading to his kitchen. Three long steps and he'd be at his minifridge. He could always reheat last night's Chinese takeout in the microwave. "Nah," he blurted, turning back to the bottle. "Too much effort."

He poured himself another glassful of whiskey and carried it out to the deck of the main tower. He leaned against the wooden railing and looked off to the horizon. One lone freighter floated in the distance, its lonely foghorn calling out to its sister ships.

There I am, Ryan thought, trying to focus on the ship's blinking runner lights. *Alone in the vast sea.*

"I had a girl," he mumbled to the water. "But she wouldn't relax and let me do anything. I mean, how can a man enjoy himself with some shrew screeching at him all the time?"

Chuckling, he knocked back another belt of whiskey. *It's better without her,* he assured himself. *That girl was an albatross around my neck.*

"Ryan, you have to stop," he mimicked in a squeaky, exaggerated falsetto. "Can't you see how you're hurting yourself?"

Ryan shook his head as he ran a shaky hand through his hair. "The only hurt I felt was in my ears from your constant harping." He finished off his drink and slammed the glass down on the wooden railing. "I'm much better off without you, Elizabeth Wakefield. That's for sure."

Ryan turned his attention to the empty beach. It was Ryan's favorite time of the day— cocktail hour. All over the West Coast he had anonymous drinking partners. He could stop feeling guilty about drinking alone.

Suddenly out of the corner of his eye he registered a flash of sun-kissed blond hair. He turned and spotted Elizabeth—or was it Jessica?—striding across the sand toward him. The woman sure walked like Jessica, proud and confident with a sexy sway to her hips, but the clothes were definitely Elizabeth's. She'd described the outfit to him when they were still talking about things other than his drinking. She was saving it for a special occasion. He'd half expected to see her wearing it the night she'd stood him up. It had to be her now.

Ryan sucked in his breath. "Welcome back, Liz," he murmured. "I guess you've decided to lighten up." His heart pounded excitedly. Judging from the way her aquamarine eyes glittered and her left cheek dimpled, she certainly didn't seem to be angry at him anymore. Suddenly he pictured himself taking her out to dinner and ordering a big porterhouse steak for two along with the restaurant's best bottle of champagne.

I don't always have to drink whiskey, he reminded himself, his stomach growling from the fantasy. *Not if Liz is going to drink with me.*

But as she reached the bottom of the wooden landing and looked up at him with her long, dark lashes fluttering mischievously, Ryan realized who it really was.

Jessica. Well, she's a much better match for the new me, he reasoned, running a hand over his face to hide his disappointment. *Nothing like a beautiful girl who knows how to live life to the fullest.*

"I hope I'm not interrupting anything," Jessica said with a bright smile. "I happened to be in the neighborhood and thought I'd stop by."

Ryan moistened his lips and grinned. "Not at all. You're just who I was hoping to see."

Chapter
Thirteen

"What a lousy day," Elizabeth muttered to herself as she stepped into the shower at the beach house. Right now what she wanted most in the world was to get cleaned up, curl up under the warm covers of her bed, and sleep for days. The fleeting relief that had come from breaking things off with Ryan had long faded. Now she was faced with another lonely evening by herself. A sob caught in her throat, and she swallowed it down.

Elizabeth sighed despondently as she turned on the shower. "Aughh," she cried, jumping back as the cold stream of water hit her squarely on the head instead of her feet. Someone had sabotaged the showerhead again. She blinked back the tears she could feel welling in her eyes. This was the last straw.

"Here," said a familiar voice. A long, deep-brown arm was reaching through the shower curtain, a towel in hand.

Elizabeth grabbed the towel and wrapped it around herself before throwing aside the curtain to find Nina heading out the bathroom door.

"Thanks," Elizabeth called, and Nina turned to face her. She hoped Nina couldn't tell it was tears trickling down her face instead of plain water.

"Same thing happened to me a half hour ago," Nina commented. "No hot water. I called maintenance, but they haven't gotten here yet."

Elizabeth groaned and put her robe on over the towel. Then both girls fell silent. A sour feeling churned in Elizabeth's stomach. She and Nina were close enough to touch, but Elizabeth felt as if there were a thick plate of glass separating them.

"Well . . . ," Nina began after a long silence. "Anyway. It'll get fixed soon."

"Yeah." Elizabeth shimmied out of the towel and rubbed it over her face and hair. Then she wrapped it around her head. All was silent for several long, painful seconds.

"OK." Nina hesitated, then headed into the hall. She sighed.

"Yes?" Elizabeth prompted. A sigh wasn't exactly a word, but it might be the prelude to the start of a conversation.

Nina shook her head. "The maintenance man didn't say when he'd be here. I guess I'll have to call him again and find out."

Elizabeth bit her lip to hide her disappointment. "I guess it couldn't hurt." She massaged her temples with her thumb and forefinger. She'd had more in-depth conversations with pets. She would have to swallow her pride and take the plunge.

"Nina—"

"Liz—"

Elizabeth felt relief flood through her as both their names rang in the air simultaneously. Obviously Nina had been bursting to say something too. Maybe there *was* hope that they could patch things up.

"You go first," Nina urged.

Elizabeth took a deep breath. "I just want you to know . . . I'm sorry about what I said the other day. You were totally right. I should have paid more attention to your problems."

Nina's face lit up in a two-hundred-watt grin. "That's exactly what I was going to say. I should have been more supportive of you too."

Elizabeth and Nina reached out and hugged each other.

"Hey, girlfriend," Nina whispered. "I missed you."

"I missed you too," Elizabeth murmured when they separated. "Now tell me everything that's been going on."

213

"Well . . . ," Nina started, suddenly looking over Elizabeth's shoulder.

Elizabeth narrowed her eyes. Was it her imagination, or was Nina hesitating? "Is something wrong?"

Nina linked her arm with Elizabeth's as they began to walk to Elizabeth's room. "Nothing I can't handle. I mean, I really can't talk about it now. I'm too confused."

"Is it the lifeguard job?"

"Partly," Nina admitted. "I'm not sure I want the job, but unless *someone* can convince Ryan to take the position back, it looks like I'm stuck with it. Like it or not."

Elizabeth ducked her head when she noticed the hopeful tone in her friend's voice. "I'm afraid I can't be much help," Elizabeth confessed. "I don't know what's happening with Ryan. He's"—she bit her lip, the words *drinking again* hanging on the tip of her tongue— "in his own world right now."

"Aren't men always like that?" Nina sat down on Elizabeth's bed. "You think you're *with* them, but then it turns out you're not with them at all. They're completely on a different planet. Weird, isn't it?"

Elizabeth nodded. It sounded as if Nina knew all about the trouble she was having with Ryan. But how could she?

214

Nina chuckled. "You know in the movies how it's always obvious which character is the bad one? You know, which one is secretly the vampire or something? But in real life you never know. Then all of sudden someone you thought you could trust is—"

"Biting your neck," Elizabeth finished for her with a weak laugh. "Are we talking about Bryan now?" she asked after a moment.

Tears came to Nina's eyes. "No . . . I mean . . . I don't know. I sort of . . . met someone. Someone who seemed really different. But I guess I was right all along. Men are just dogs."

"Do you want to talk about it?"

"No, I'd rather not," Nina said, crying and laughing all at the same time. "It's too horrible and humiliating to discuss with anyone but a total stranger."

Elizabeth laughed. "I know exactly what you mean." When it came to Ryan, she'd be more willing to seek the advice of an anonymous counselor on a telephone help line than one of her closest friends.

"I wish I could tell you about it, Liz, but I can't."

"You don't have to tell me the details," she said softly. "My only advice is to trust your heart."

Nina shrugged. "After what Bryan did to me at the beginning of the summer . . . I'm afraid to trust myself. Once burned, twice shy."

215

"Maybe you shouldn't judge all guys because of what Bryan did."

"You're probably right," Nina mumbled, picking at a piece of fuzz on the quilt covering the bed. "But enough about me. What about you? What's going on with you and Ryan?"

Elizabeth looked past Nina guiltily. "I blew up at him this morning," she admitted, wincing at the memory.

"Why?" Nina asked. "What did he do?"

Elizabeth sighed and took the towel off her head. Nina was her best friend. Would it really be so awful to tell *her* about Ryan's drinking?

Only if betraying his confidence is no problem for you, a little voice told her.

No, she argued. *Nina has her reasons for keeping quiet, and unfortunately so do I.*

Elizabeth cleared her throat. "Ryan's having . . . personal problems. And instead of letting me help him, he's pushing me away," Elizabeth said, her voice faltering slightly. Shoving her away was more like it.

"So what are you going to do?"

"Not what I'm *going* to do—what I *did*. I ended it." She wrapped her arms around her trembling body and hugged herself.

Nina squeezed her arm gently. "And now you feel differently?"

Elizabeth nodded and with a shaky hand

wiped a tear from the corner of her eye. "I don't know. Maybe I was too tough. Ryan is going through a lot, and I should have known better. Anger is never the way to handle a situation, even if it does give you a temporary sense of empowerment."

Nina sighed. "It's always easier to figure that out after the fact, isn't it?"

"Mm-hmm," Elizabeth agreed, but her big question remained unanswered. "What do you think, Nina? Should I give him another chance?"

"Well, if you talk to Ryan, then maybe I won't have to keep this head lifeguard position after all," Nina offered.

Elizabeth smirked. "Do I detect a hint of the mercenary here?"

Giggling, Nina patted her on the back. "I still have your best interests at heart. I can tell you're not over Ryan yet."

Elizabeth smiled. She couldn't deny it. "I'll try to talk to him one more time."

"You do that." Nina got up and headed for the bedroom door. "I bet you'll be surprised."

"We're missing a beautiful sunset," Jessica called teasingly to Ryan, feeling his eyes burning into her from the other side of the main tower. She hadn't intended to hang around for more than a few minutes, but the appreciation on

Ryan's handsome face had made her lose all track of time.

Jessica stretched her long, bare arms lazily. Through the narrow cracks in the blinds she could make out glimmers of the bright pinks, blues, and purples from the setting sun. "Maybe I should open the shades."

Ryan smiled from where he sat straddling a hard chair. He rested his chin on his toned forearms. "Who needs the sunset when I've got the moon and the stars right here?"

Jessica giggled and shifted her position in the wide leather captain's chair for a better view. "But won't nature's beauty add even more to the evening?"

Ryan shook his head. "She can't hold a candle to you."

"Then how come I'm here and you're way over there?"

Ryan stood up with the sexy grace of a jaguar and sauntered over to stand behind her. He bent down low until his lips grazed her hair. "I'm trying to be on my best behavior."

Jessica shivered as his warm, tangy breath tickled her ear.

"Cold?" he murmured. His strong hands moved down from the back of the chair to her barely concealed shoulders. One of his hands moved up and massaged the nape of her neck.

Goose bumps shot across her arms while a jolt of heat turned her cheeks a bright pink. She turned to look at him, her lips slightly parted. "I'm getting hotter by the moment."

Ryan ran a finger gently along her jawline. "Maybe I should go back to my seat?"

Jessica raised one perfectly sculpted eyebrow and smiled. "Not so fast . . . I feel another chill coming on."

Ryan laughed. "Do you think this chair's big enough for the two of us?"

Jessica narrowed her eyes playfully. "It would make a tight fit."

Ryan stepped around the chair so that he stood before her. As she looked up at his muscular chest, every ripple visible under the thin cotton of his T-shirt, she could feel her pulse begin to race and her heart start slamming against her rib cage.

"Maybe too tight," he whispered seductively. "There's a lot more space in my room."

Jessica squeezed the arms of the chair. *Is this all wrong?* she wondered. She wasn't sure if it was the enclosed room or the heat of her own body that was making her head spin. She took a deep breath and tried to steady herself. *I'd better stop this before it goes any further.*

Ryan reached down and pulled her to her feet. "Come on," he whispered.

Jessica took a tentative step on shaky legs. Before she could move another muscle, he swept her up in his arms, his mouth passionately seeking hers. Jessica resisted for only a second. In a dizzying moment of abandon she felt her lips and the rest of her body yield to his. She was lost, her mind reeling at a million miles per hour, her lips fitting perfectly with his.

I've wanted Ryan to kiss me like this from the moment I laid eyes on him, she realized as he molded his muscular body to hers. The urgency of his kisses frightened and thrilled her. Her hands found the back of his neck and she pulled him even closer, tasting the sea and something else—something hot and sweet—on his lips and tongue. *Don't let it stop,* she thought. *Make it last forever.*

Finally, almost faint from the intensity of his embrace, she pulled back to catch her breath. "Ryan!" she exclaimed, pushing lightly on his chest. "I never knew you noticed me."

Jessica could read the desire blazing in Ryan's eyes, but like a gentleman, he gently placed her back on her feet and dropped his hands from around her waist. "I've noticed you plenty of times," he growled. "How could I miss someone so beautiful?"

"Then don't stop," she whispered, pressing her body tightly against his and running her hands through his soft, sun-streaked brown hair. "Kiss me again."

Ryan obliged, pressing his lips to hers tenderly before he scooped her up and carried her into his room. They tumbled onto the bed, his strong arms clasping her to his chest, their hearts beating as one.

He's all mine, she realized, her lips mingling with his as she unleashed all her built-up passion. *I'm not in anyone's shadow anymore!*

"It's times like this that I wish I had a car," Nina whispered as she pedaled her bike toward SeaMist Island. To spend another second apart from Stu seemed almost unbearable. Now that she'd made up her mind to go talk to him, she could hardly contain herself.

Nina stood on her pedals as she sailed over the bridge. The wind whipped through her hair. She practically flew up the driveway and dismounted with an excited leap. She could see Stu lying in his hammock under two palm trees. His eyes were closed, and his mouth was slightly parted in sleep.

Nina longed to press her lips to his and gently kiss him awake. She walked stealthily toward him. But as she bent down to press her lips to his, he awoke.

"Nina," he said softly, the corners of his eyes

crinkling happily. "You came back." He opened his arms wide and Nina fell into his embrace, her unexpected weight toppling the hammock, sending them both tumbling onto the wispy grass below.

Stu laughed as he brushed the sand from her hair. They lay together, entangled on the ground. "I missed you, mermaid," he murmured huskily before covering her face with kisses.

"I missed you too, but . . ." Nina pulled away, her heart pounding. "I need you to tell me the truth. Do you really mean all those things you said?"

Stu's eyes never wavered from hers for a moment. "Yes," he said solemnly. "I love *you*, Nina Harper. There's nobody else."

Nina's heart poured over with tenderness. "I'm sorry I didn't believe you." Her lips met his, and they fused into a deep, passionate kiss. Nina felt a delicious tingle radiating from where Stu's strong hands held her. She felt a glowing warmth traveling through her entire body. Her suspicious thoughts melted away—discounted and forgotten—as she felt nothing but love pulsing between them.

A soft rustle in the reeds behind them made Nina jump. "Did you hear that?" she asked, sitting up.

Stu gave her a crooked smile. "I can't hear anything but my own pulse."

Nina laughed and fell back into his arms, bliss quickly overtaking her as his mouth gently explored hers.

Stu broke away suddenly. "Wait—I did hear something." There was a hint of alarm in his blue eyes as he searched the clumps of tall reeds around them.

Nina felt the small hairs on the back of her neck stand up. "Is something out there?" she whispered.

Stu narrowed his eyes. "I don't know. But I'm going to check it out." He jumped to his feet.

"Wait for me," Nina called, scrambling after him. There was no way she wanted to be left alone right now. She clung to his arm as they slowly made their way toward the reeds.

Nina screamed as a large, dark mass darted out of its hiding place in the beach grass.

"It's OK, Nina," Stu assured her. "It's just a raccoon."

"Oh!" Nina laughed in relief. "Thank goodness."

Stu grinned and wrapped her in his arms. "So much for our gate-crasher," he whispered in her hair. "Look. She has pups." He pointed to two baby raccoons scampering behind the big one.

Nina giggled as she watched the little fluff balls tumble on top of each other. She looked up at Stu, her eyes shining, and threw her arms around his neck. Once again she let herself drift away in a soul-searching kiss.

Finally, coming up for air, they broke away. Nina had turned to head back to the hammock when suddenly, as if out of nowhere, a bizarre-looking woman with a shock of white-blond hair stood in front of the hammock as if she had been there all along. Nina's eyes widened in shock. She was no more than three feet away from them!

Nina let out a terrified shriek and instinctively threw her arms around Stu.

The blonde's face twisted into a hideous scowl. "Get your hands off him," she hissed furiously.

Nina whimpered, recoiling from the woman's look of seething hatred. Something about her face seemed familiar. *That's it—she's the woman who was staring at me on the beach this morning,* she realized. But there was more to it than that. She'd seen her—known her—long before that. Those almond-shaped eyes . . .

"Rachel!" Stu hollered.

"Rachel *Max!*" Nina yelled. She couldn't believe how different she looked. Rachel's dark hair had been cut short and bleached; the snide smirk that had been perpetually on her lips was now replaced by something more disturbing—something evil. "What do you want?"

"Want?" Rachel took a step toward them.

"What's mine, of course . . . Stuart."

Stu stood in front of Nina. "This is the girl I was telling you about," he said over his shoulder.

Rachel cackled. "See, Nina? I'm never far from Stuart's thoughts."

Nina's mouth dropped open. "This is impossible. You're supposed to be in prison."

"Prison?" Stu shouted.

Rachel put her hands on her hips indignantly. "I did my time. Now get your hands off my man."

Nina squeezed Stu's biceps tighter. "He's not your man, Rachel. He's mine." She released him and took a step forward. Now *she* was standing protectively in front of *Stu*.

"Don't push me, lifeguard," Rachel threatened, clenching her fists, the tendons in her arms standing out. "Pedal on home like a good little girl, or it'll be more than your bike tires and bathing suits I cut up."

Nina gasped. "So it was you all along—the bike tires, the bathing suits, the doll in the water—I bet you even knocked me out in my own room! How *dare* you do this to me!"

Rachel threw back her head and laughed. "Just protecting my territory. Now . . . go . . . *away!*" She lunged toward Nina in a violent rage.

Stu jumped between them, holding Rachel off. "Nina's not going anywhere, Rachel. *You*

225

are." He pushed her back a few feet. "Can't you take a hint? There's nothing between us."

Rachel's thin lips curled into a cruel smile. "I'm afraid that's where you're wrong, Stuart." She rubbed her belly gently. "We're joined in the most precious thing a man and a woman can share. A miracle."

Nina felt her mouth turn dry and her temples begin to pound. Stu's next words seemed to come from far off, as if he'd already been torn from her life.

"What do you mean?" he asked.

"What do I mean?" Rachel giggled. "I mean I'm *pregnant*, Stuart. I'm going to have your baby!"

"I've *got* to make Ryan understand that I'm trying to help him," Elizabeth whispered to herself as she strode along the wooden walkway toward the main tower. "And I can't let my emotions get the better of me if he tries to push me away again."

She looked nervously over her shoulder toward the beach house. *Am I doing the right thing?* she wondered. She shivered and wrapped her cotton sweater tighter around her thin summer dress.

"If I'm going to talk to Ryan, I have to choose my words carefully," she told herself.

"With the way he's acting, even a hint of criticism could be enough to put him on the attack."

Or send him off on another drinking binge, she silently argued.

"But how can I make him see how self-destructive he's being without criticizing him?" she asked herself despairingly.

Elizabeth rested her elbows on the walkway's wooden railing and looked out at the deserted beach. There was only one way to get it right: practice. She closed her eyes and mentally pictured Ryan sitting before her.

"Ryan, I'll support you—whatever you're going through—no matter how long it takes."

Elizabeth's body jerked as she realized what she'd just said. "No matter how long it takes?" she echoed. "What am I saying? Who wants to be tied down to an active alcoholic?" She gripped the side of the railing. What if Ryan's alcoholism was so bad he *couldn't* stop drinking?

"This is Ryan Taylor you're talking about," she reminded herself. "He got sober once; he can do it again."

But will he? Elizabeth wondered. *What if he decides never to get sober?*

Elizabeth grimaced and ducked under the railing, jumping off the walkway onto the sandy beach. "With these negative thoughts I won't do either of us any good." She gazed out at the riot of color splashed across the horizon by the last rays of the setting sun.

Too bad Ryan can't be here with me now, she thought. At the beginning of the summer they'd reunited while watching a romantic sunset just like this one. She could almost smell Ryan's clean, fresh skin and feel the warm pressure of his arms around her. But if Ryan were here right now, what would she say?

"That I'm in his corner!" Elizabeth said aloud. *That's it!* she thought, turning in the sand and heading for the main tower.

"Ryan," she began again. "I'll leave you alone if that's what you want." She felt hot tears build behind her eyes at the thought. She swallowed hard and forced herself to be strong. "I hope you'll still include me in your life." She dabbed at her eyes with the sleeve of her sweater. "But if you want to have fun for a while—" She hesitated. "If you want to stop drinking, I'll support you."

And what if I don't? she imagined him asking.

"If you don't, I'll still be there for you. No matter what," she whispered as she approached the darkened main tower.

That's all I can do, she realized. *All I can do is love him—and let him figure his life out on his own.*

Elizabeth frowned and checked her watch. Why were the main tower lights off? It was barely 8 P.M. *Has he turned in for the night already?* she wondered. She was sure Ryan would have passed by her on the walkway if he'd gone out for the evening.

She increased her pace, anxiety suddenly replacing her newfound resolve. *What if something happened?* she worried. *He might have passed out with the stove on. Or stumbled and hit his head.* She began running, her ponytail streaming out behind her.

Elizabeth pushed open the front door of the main tower and snapped on the lights. The room was empty. She looked around, glancing over at the shift schedule on the wall above the desk and the CPR instruction posters. All quiet.

"Mmm."

Her ears perked up as she heard a low groan. *That sound came from Ryan's room,* she thought with a start. With a trembling hand she pushed open the door that led to Ryan's living quarters and stepped through. The noise was coming from his bedroom, and it was getting louder as she approached. Was he snoring? Choking? She was dizzy with anxiety.

She took the two steps along the short hallway and gingerly turned the doorknob to his living quarters. She would come back in the morning if Ryan was asleep. She didn't want to wake him. But she had to make sure that he was OK.

She cracked the door open, bit by bit, the diffuse light from the hallway seeping slowly in behind her and illuminating the tiny room.

As Elizabeth looked in, she felt her eyes widen and her mouth fall open.

No! Her throat constricted violently.

No! She felt herself plunging into the blackest hole imaginable.

No! Her heart fell and shattered into a million pieces.

The moaning she'd heard hadn't been Ryan in distress. Anything but. It had been the sound of Ryan's impassioned sighs as he kissed another woman who sat curled up in his lap!

Elizabeth gasped in shock and staggered backward, closing her eyes to blot out the terrible scene before her. The slender body in the all-too-familiar white outfit . . . the long blond hair flowing over her shoulders . . . arms wrapped possessively around his neck . . . lips hungrily exploring his mouth . . . like she wasn't even there . . .

No.

No, it can't be . . .

Elizabeth pulled the door shut silently, clutching at the hallway wall to keep from collapsing. All her nerve endings seemed to be crying out, echoing the grief pouring through her veins. She buried her face in her hands as she dashed out of the main tower, ran down to the beach, and fell to her knees in the sand. "This is all my fault!" she sobbed. "I practically pushed them together. But I didn't mean to. I didn't!"

Now that Jessica finally has Ryan to herself, will she remain on top of the world—or be in more danger than ever? Find out in Sweet Valley University #32, THE BOYS OF SUMMER.

SIGN UP FOR THE
SWEET VALLEY HIGH®
FAN CLUB!

Hey, girls! Get all the gossip on Sweet
Valley High's® most popular teenagers
when you join our fantastic Fan Club!
As a member, you'll get all of this really
cool stuff:

- Membership Card with your own
  personal Fan Club ID number
- A Sweet Valley High® Secret
  Treasure Box
- Sweet Valley High® Stationery
- Official Fan Club Pencil (for secret
  note writing!)
- Three Bookmarks
- A "Members Only" Door Hanger
- Two Skeins of J. & P. Coats® Embroidery
  Floss with flower barrette instruction
  leaflet

- Two editions of *The Oracle* newsletter
- Plus exclusive Sweet Valley High®
  product offers, special savings,
  contests, and much more!
